DESTRUCTION
OF
EARTH

DESTRUCTION OF EARTH

ROBERT REYNOLDS

DESTRUCTION OF EARTH

iUniverse books may be ordered through booksellers or by contacting:

iUniverse
1663 Liberty Drive
Bloomington, IN 47403
www.iuniverse.com
844-349-9409

ISBN: 978-1-6632-0820-0 (sc)
ISBN: 978-1-6632-0821-7 (e)

Print information available on the last page.

iUniverse rev. date: 09/16/2020

AUTHOR'S NOTE

When reading over each of these stories came an idea to bring together a possible scenario that might have happened if we ever wanted to see if our lives could be different in many ways. It does not take a person without creativity to see anyone can have the imagination to pull any of their works together and make something great out of them. So please if any of you have dreams that can be drawn together and make something great please by all means necessary do so and see what you or even a group can come up with to enrich the world with your talents.

DEDICATION

To the most beautiful women in my life that have shown me, how to continue even during my life struggles and they are Paula and Dena. They are very smart, beautiful women in the world that need to be recognized in a very particular way.

CHAPTER

1

IN THE BEGINNING, WE all have some understanding about why we are here on Earth, but sometimes that understanding is not enough to stop any global destruction from happening in our life times. With this thought comes the true reality of how our own destiny would either doom us or bring forth salvation to mankind. When humans first showed up in the scheme of things they knew nothing of what was in store for them in the distant future. As mankind started to form thought from the beginning an understanding grew towards the future of humanity. Throughout the ages of man, we have found many different ways to destroy things in our world. Over the thousands of years we became aware of how to survive the harsh environments by destroying or taking from others to ensure our own survival. Each of us has big fears that we try to confront on a daily basis when the moment and time are right for humanity. What truly comes from our fears in life brings forth hatred in some, but love in others of how out fears stem from raw emotions of everyday life events. Killing or causing the death of someone you love in life can be harmful to the soul. With other fears that people have in life are illnesses, diseases and also aging comes with an understanding we all must die at some point during our lives.

Another thing that people fear are wars, shipwrecks and other disasters around the world because of love ones that die. the first in many steps of facing our fears is to understand them and also to deal with them head on. Killing someone in life is hard for the average person in the world, but when it comes to greed, suspicions, and technology it all goes out the window. Greed can lead anyone towards killing someone if the price is right. Yes, it is true we all look at each other in various ways and says to ourselves about the different suspicions about everybody we encounter on a daily basis. Which leads us to the next reason for killing someone and that is technology. All of these items can motivate someone to kill a love one, but in truth one option needs to be understood and that is when someone is dying a slow painful death. After this, it will lead towards disasters that we face on a daily basis due to human malfunctions or weather related plus some cosmic understanding with otherworldly disasters from an alien race far, far away from us.

This leads us to the different types of disasters and they are death, thunder and lightning, the dark, lies, murder, crime of passion, wars, wrecked spaceships and even the unknown disasters. Each one of these will lead to conclusions about our world, but two of them can lead us in a direction that nobody wants to admit towards because of reality it shows. True the first few only deals with people on Earth but the last two is the main issue and part of this story that I want to focus on. There have been some unexplained things that have happened over the years and centuries on Earth. Which leads us into the heart of this story that is being told by one of the survivors that were left alive, uninfected and unharmed by the alien creature?

This story pertains to three different stories that have been foretold or even foreseen, but to fully witness the destruction of each one can show each of us how we are able to survive. The first of the three stories was called "The Plague," in which killed about ten to twenty million people in Europe. The second of the three stories is called "Mysterious Cylinder," in which unleashed a creature of an unknown origin upon the world. The third and final of the three stories is "Large size meteor that struck the Earth," and when it did hit the Earth it once again unleashed hell onto this world.

Some people may think these different stories are true in every way, but some of the information is true but the others are from my imagination. Explaining how each one of these stories can be intertwined so easily that one might think it could or even would happen to our world. The first would be "The Plague," in which yes it has reappeared every few decades in new areas to cause more harm to people. Finally, the last sighting of the plague was in the new land which will soon be called America. The second would be "Mysterious Cylinder," in which is oddly enough found in the same location as where the plague had ended and vanished from sight. Now the strange and weird part of this story is that of 'Texas Size Meteor," in which now has many different scientists trying to understand why the impact coordinates are the same location as "The Plague" and "Mysterious Cylinder." One may think how it is possible and what could be attracting such destruction in our world.

If each of these stories comes to pass it would seem that this world could be a target by an unknown Alien Race. Which is one of many possibilities that have crossed many conspiracy people minds, but also it leads scientists to believe that something or someone is trying to kill them all. Everybody has many theories as to why all of these legends might be true, but only one has full knowledge of why this is happening in the world. When a person connects the dots throughout history from the plague to the meteors missing Earth but eventually that person is led to the conclusion all three legends will happen in the past, present or future of our world. A question to any person seeking the understanding of any of these legends must first open one's mind to the possibility that our planet may be doomed. If that understanding is finally realized in every way and we then must understand that we may not be alone in this world or even in this galaxy. Now, this may lead people to believe that there has to be a modern day explanation of all the three legends.

Oh sure everything in this world can be explained that is old or new by some old story plus wives tales throughout the years. Yes, some of the old stories have been passed down from generation to generation. Some stories are true and others are made up to scare children into behaving properly while growing up in life. People always try to tell stories about how if they do not behave a monster will eat them. When a child grows up believing in stories and fairy tales that has been passed down through the family, but once in a while, a person needs to search for the truth behind the stories and fairy tales. When the time comes there has to be someone to search for clues to find out if stories and fairy tales are true. This story is about the different stories and also the one person that searches for the truth in everything that surrounds us in this world.

One major question that needs to be answered is how or why did these events occur in the world? It is not a simple question to answer because since the dawn of time we are a race that wants to expand our minds, but we also want to understand why we are here in the first place. What was the plan for mankind to exist in this world, but also why do we need to explore every inch of this world and including space? To fully explore these questions one must fully explore oneself because of how we act and see each other. To fully explore the reasons behind these three legends is to fully explore the reasons why this world and all other planets were created in the first place.

There have been inventors, authors, scientists, dreamers and even artists plus others that are not named has wondered if we are alone in this vast expanse of a galaxy. Another question for us is it the knowledge we seek or is it to conquer other worlds that is out there in space. To answer this question is to fully see how far our world has come to be when it was first born billions of years ago. There are people that say we were born from Adam and Eve but other say we were born from the ooze that was on our planet from the beginning of the creation of our world.

The truth is unknown but most people would be very interested in why we were created but as we go through time the believing in one option does not lead to the other option. The Bible states we come from Adam and Eve. But many people say we come from evolution throughout time from when the world was created until the time man was created to roam the world. In truth this debate has gone on for a very long time but what is the true answer to this debate is unknown. What if we are not alone and we finally find out there are other habitual worlds in other galaxies.

The knowledge and understanding that newspaper articles can show us our own future help each one of us to believe or not to believe depending on our beliefs. For all the different people that believe in many great things that have happened since time began. That in itself leads many people to truly believe we are doomed to repeat all things until nothing is left. The next logical step would be to take steps in safeguarding and also the protection for Earth. In order to do so, we must first have the proper technology to protect the population of Earth. Thus leads some of us to advance all studies to acquire all technology at a fast pace but sometimes it is not fast enough. This leads certain people to take matters into their own hands for the safety of their family and themselves.

A company that is researching to find new ways of curing the different diseases and viruses that is in our world. One researcher named Robert Maxwell stumbled upon a small article that talks about three different stories that can destroy our world. Robert went to his boss to explain what he has found buried deep in the newspaper archives. His boss told Robert to find something useful or he would be fired by the end of the week. Robert worked for the next week by researching all newspaper archives for any articles about the different stories. On the very last day of researching Robert finally found what he was looking for, and it showed how the information could be used to develop many cures for certain diseases and viruses around the world. When Robert gathered the information to show his boss after his lunch break, and that is when he found his boss dead. To explain more about Robert Maxwell, his favorite pass time is reading about history, science, art and even criminal stories that were written throughout history. He also has a Bachelors in Criminal Justice but found doing research during his classes Robert has become more interested in the background information about how certain things throughout history is intertwined with each other. His passion is to truly uncover something great that everybody has missed or trying to prove once and for all that he is worthy of being an intelligent person to his friends and family.

On Robert's understanding of the different articles in the newspaper archives left many unanswered questions in his mind because of the many stories about how the three stories around the world were created to cause fear among the people in the world. For reasons that are only known to the company for researching these stories is to see if any other explanations could be found for the causes of the diseases and viruses around the world in our lifetime. Robert has tried a lot of things to figure out what needs to be done to see if any of these things are true, but in order to do so, he would have to travel to the town where he suspects the events had occurred throughout history.

One might ask us how long and how far should one go for knowledge and understanding for mankind. In the research Robert realized that each of these different articles shows us how diseases, viruses, mysterious objects and even meteors are trying to wipe out all life on our planet. The first article that Robert found was about the black plague that appeared in 1347 during the month of October. The article led Robert to further study the different diseases and viruses across the world.

CHAPTER
2

AFTER READING AND STUDYING the newspaper article about the plague Robert realized one important fact about the articles. It leads to the understanding of how some of the old diseases and viruses came about into the world. When the plague first arrived in Europe upon a ship from a foreign land in which more and more people it comes into contact within Europe. As the plague spreads across Europe the people could not imagine what would happen if they ever came across something like this in their lifetime. The plague came before the knowledge and understanding what it was in the first place because of how little things were known in the medical field at the time. After the plague infected the people it encountered first it spread across Europe in which it went unchecked and began to infect a lot more people in the process.

The people started to believe it was a curse from God but in reality the real reason behind the plague was still a mystery depending on who you ask during that time period. As the plague spreads across Europe all people could do was to watch and do nothing because nobody understood why this was happening to them. As the plague spreads from one village to the next infecting people as it continues to go unchecked in the world. In watching the plague infect people from the different villages across Europe they also noticed it causes other symptoms in each person differently because of how the plague attacks the body. With the population slowly being reduced because of the plague which started in 1347 by what was thought to be rats later on in the investigation. Noticing how the old diseases and viruses were being diagnosed by the herbalist and the under-educated doctors at the time. Yes, it is true that the knowledge from that time period was lacking, to say the least. Without fully realizing how horrific the plague could be because how it causes certain things in the body to happen. In a strange way it causes a chain reaction within the body and changes it to something else entirely. Knowing and understanding how it affects a person body is very complicated and plus being unknown to the best of professionals in that time period.

In that situation for stopping or containing the disease or virus becomes great in order to save the world from harm. This leads to forming a special group to chase the main reason for the plague being in the world. It will take finding the right people that will know how to deal with the plague. Each person for the must has at least one or more specialty to be in the group. The people in the group must be the top in their fields because of the unknown terrain they will be facing. Firstly, is the chemist and biologist that are combined together for studying the effects of the infection on the new host? Secondly, would be the survivalist and guide for the unknown terrain during their travels. Thirdly, would be a doctor to study how each new victim was infected by the plague. Lastly, would be an engineer because the person needs the understanding of trapping the cause of the plague and keep it away from the population in the world. Each one of these people must understand that this mission is only a one-way mission with no possibilities for returning home to family and friends.

The group is trying to locate the source of the plague that started in Europe and caused sickness across most of the Europe. They started by traveling to the small rural villages that were infected by the plague and followed it around the country. Even after the weeks of traveling and searching the different villages for the source of the plague. It led the group to a small village next to a sea shore and this village held the ship builders for small boats to large boats for transportation. The group slowly enters into the village and noticed everyone they met was infected, but also, they needed to burn all the buildings and food supplies to and eliminate all traces of the infected people. With the few people that were uninfected by the plague boarded a single transport ship and set sail across the Atlantic Ocean away from the remnants of the plague behind them and now is the time to follow the plague across the ocean.

As they traveled the vast ocean they needed supplies for the voyage to ensure survival. After the short time in the small fishing village, the group traveled for nine years and no trace of the plague. As the group travels, they learn and study new ways of doing things to help them in their adventures. The new knowledge of the different techniques plus new technologies learned from the areas they visited during their travels shows them how much the world has changed over the years. The ship and the people aboard reached a new land mass that was unknown to all of them. In realizing this they had to find somewhere to go ashore to relocate the source of the plague again.

Slowly moving towards inland in search of the plague but realizing they were too late to save anyone. The plague had changed into another infectious disease. As the group followed the string of people dying and realizing they were not prepared at all for what is coming in the near future. The people of the new land are very different from the people that live in Europe. The differences between both types of society are so vast the understanding is the same with the knowledge of the world is changing. Within the first few weeks of exploring the new land, they were noticing how hard it is in tracking down the plague again. It took another two weeks before they finally picked up the trail again for reasons that are unknown to them. This time around they had to do the same thing as before and that is to burn the bodies, buildings plus all of the food supplies that were infected. Over the years, they followed the trail of the plague, but also, they realized it will take a long time to accomplish their mission. The main reason for this is simple, and that reason is they had to stay away from the local natives of the new land so they will not be influenced by their actions. The group fears that they are nowhere close to catching the cause of the plague. Nine years plus has now passed from the plague first hit the shores of Europe and now another two years has passed afterward so in total eleven years in all. For the next twenty years, they traveled all over the new land to learn and study along the way to ensure the safety of the world's population. Now is the time to find a way to ensure the capture and the containing of the plague until someone or something can finally kill the cause for good. Slowly one by one of the main group dies but before they did they shared their knowledge with the new people that had joined the group from the small village that where the shipbuilders lived in Europe.

As the new people learned the adventures skills they knew one day that the time will come to be on their own. The younger adventure needs to find mates that will obey to the secrecy because no one needs to know about the source of the plague. For the next one hundred years, it will be passed down from generation to generation for this mission needs to be done. It will take that long to ensure the knowledge and skills are capable enough to trap and contain the source of the plague. This time, it will take another twenty years to gain the knowledge and understanding why this needs to happen for the world. Finally, after one hundred and thirty-one years of traveling the group realized they have been chasing the cause of the plague all this time. The main reason they realized this is that the plague had changed to something else but still had the same symptoms and reactions as the previous sightings. The group settled down in what will be called New Mexico in years to come, but beforehand they had found a nice spot along the southern area of the lower mountain range.

Time is getting close to ending the plague, old diseases, and viruses that had traveled all the way from Europe. The cruel fate of the world has been foretold and foreseen even before the dawn of time began. The construction began with new and old process techniques for building the secret bunker for containing the cause of old and new diseases plus viruses from Europe to the new land. The knowledge and learning for the future technology that is needed for the secret bunker came with a price and that price knows that nobody will know what they did for the world. The construction is moving right along for the timetable that was set far in advance, but also, the time is growing short for the group to capture the cause of the plague.

Finally, the cause of the plague appeared close to them and it was time to capture it for the purpose of protecting the world from harm. Now is the time to trap it but something weird has happened it is not a small rodent. It was an alien creature that showed up around the small town that was also constructed around the secret bunker. It took a week to finally capture plus in addition they froze the alien creature so it could no longer harm anyone in the world. They all took precaution around the alien creature as to ensure nobody gets infected by the alien creature. The alien creature followed one of the people from the small town into a cave that was prepared for the alien creature far in advance. Once the alien creature entered the cave the person exited out a secret tunnel that was dug up for the purpose of escaping the cave and the alien creature. An electrified fence was activated to trap the alien creature until it was time to move the alien creature into the secret bunker.

The building of the underground secret bunker with all the new technologies for the purpose of containing the alien creature is going as planned. In learning and using the new process for ensuring the metal was indestructible until the time was right. During that time, the bunker is to be watched from a far enough distance that nobody knows it is there in the first place. The secret bunker has one way in and one way out so it cannot be located on any map or by any person searching the area that is new to the location.

The next phase of the construction on the secret bunker and that will be the cryogenic chamber. With this type of technology, it all came from another time period from the future. The understanding and knowledge that has been passed down from generation to generation were first taught by five teachers from the future. It was unknown at the time that this knowledge will ever be needed but now is the time to use this knowledge to safeguard mankind from harm. Also ensuring the new technology is not discovered by anyone else at the right time.

Now one person must keep watch over the alien creature and the secret bunker under the ground not too far from the mountain range.

In the understanding that only one person is allowed in the secret bunker with the alien creature at a time for the reason only known to the protectors of Earth. In doing so that person will make sure nothing goes wrong will all the controls of the secret bunker and the cryogenic chamber. Over the years, the world will move on until it is time to be done. In the years ahead leads the people to understand that the knowledge is the key to protecting the future of the world. It will take years to ensure that nothing should go wrong with the secret bunker and the alien creature.

CHAPTER

3

WITHIN THE NEWSPAPER ARTICLE it had a small side note about an old mysterious diary that held clues about what had happened during the 16th century in the new land. It was rumored that the diary was nothing but a hoax, because there was no way it could be real. Also further down the article it gives a small reference to the diary by Hannah Smith. The reference was only in the article to prove some partial truth about the diary but in knowing this does not ensure that it is real in the first place. The diary is written by a little girl named Hannah Smith and her travels in the new land. The strange thing about the diary is the mention about the secret bunker plus traveling between the five small villages around the secret bunker. While Hannah was young she also traveled high above the mountain top range to understand the complex meaning for becoming a protector of Earth.

The biggest problem about the diary is that nobody could in fact produce the diary for inspection and to have it authenticated. So whatever people wrote about it just shows how little they knew about the diary and its true intent for the world. While searching for clues any clues about the diary Robert realized beside the reference in the article and the link that were the only two things that showed anything about the diary in total. Without the diary the logical step would be is to see what other records showing for Hannah Smith. While searching all the documents he could online and strangely enough it only showed the two links. Then Robert saw another link to a poem that was published in the mid 1950's. It was called Protectors of Earth plus it was written in English. That was only half of the strange thing because the people that published that poem said Hannah Smith is 85 years old at the time. That cannot be right at all so it would figure the next step would be is to make a family tree for Hannah Smith.

After seeing the age of this Hannah Smith something does not add up but now is the time to order or download the poem to see what it holds. While doing this Robert tries to do a family tree for Hannah Smith and has no luck because of how or where should he start to find clues about her family. The outcome was starting to become very difficult in finding any information about her family and also including herself. As he was searching for any records about her parents to see if they had any other children and no luck with that either. When Robert was trying to map out her family blood line since there are no records and now he had to try another way in finding out who was her family was during her lifetime.

Since Robert could not find anything about Hannah Smith family blood line it was now time to check out the professional line from the modern to the past. In doing so he noticed a pattern with the names of each chemist throughout the ages. The funny but strange thing of all was his own mother had the same maiden last name as Hannah Smith mother because Hannah's mother married name was Scott. With some understanding for certain name change it shows how Hannah's family blood line branches off in only three different ways. First way goes to the chemists, second way goes to the doctors and the third way goes to biology so it shows how her family stays with science and nothing else.

This leads him to full realization that he is a descendant of Hannah Smith. In doing this it lead him to his parents that for some strange reason were not chemist but normal people. In realizing that he is part of this story because of the family line and it lead Robert to think about how he would not have found out if his own company did not hire him to do research. What is truly surprising with everything is how little Robert knew about his family blood line even from his own parents. A little part of him knew something was a little wrong when his parents told him nothing about their past for reasons that are unclear even to him.

It prompted him to call his parents to ask some very hard questions about their own blood line. By calling his parents he found out yes it is true about his great-grandparents were chemists. Robert mother told him, "I will be sending you something in the mail to look at during your next pit stop on your journey. Why are you sending my something to look at when you can just tell me over the phone? The funny thing is what was said next dumbfounded even Robert that his own mother would say this out loud. Robert's mother said, "I am not allowed to say it over the phone but I will tell you this please be careful while on the road during your journey my son.

Soon the truth about Robert's blood line will be revealed fully and why his own understanding about this journey is so great to be on right now. The knowledge will show how this story and him are related in every sense of the word, but also the correlation between these stories and Robert will eventual come to head for reasons beyond our imagination. Compared to the imagination of a child to an adult all depends on how they look at things in the world. The understanding on how each of us look at things in the world can change the way we imagine how certain events can affects us as a whole but also how it can destroy us as an individual. Our own family blood line can merge with others in the world even if we are not related in any other way.

When Robert stopped at the next pit stop on his journey and somehow a mysterious package was waiting for him by the time he checked into the hotel. After arriving at the hotel and once he said his name the front desk clerk said you have a package waiting for you. I will go get it and be right back with it sir. He remembered his mother saying that she will be sending a package to him at his next pit stop on his journey. After checking into his room he took his package from his parents to the room. He set everything down and went to the small desk in front of the hotel room window. Robert sits down and looks at the package but also has this feeling of being watched over his shoulder. He slowly opens the mysterious package from his parents and saw Hannah Smith's diary staring back at him.

After Robert opened the mysterious package from his parents and realizing it was Hannah Smith diary it dawned on him that everything was true. He then realized by opening the diary that everything was in code. It was not just any simple code that could or can be cracked it was a code that had no deciphering code that goes with it. On every single page of the diary it was full of code with unknown language or symbols. The unknown language or symbols are from any dead languages that are no longer known in the world. Robert is one step closer to the secrets of when the first articles were read about the plague that had caused so many people to die in Europe.

Robert got a phone call from his mother in which told him that his uncle had died in a car crash on the very same day he arrived at the hotel and received the mysterious package. Later that day he wanted something to eat at the restaurant down the road but as he went to his car and tried to start his car it would not even start at all. Instead his car went ka-boom and part of the engine went out through the hood of the car. So now he has to call a tow truck to come get his car and have a mechanic to try and fix it for his journey. The funny thing is it was kind of expected because of how his uncle had died in a car crash. One thing after another has gone wrong and he still is only halfway to his goal but also he has something to report back to his company. Later after his car was towed away and he called for take-out to be delivered to his hotel room. Robert finally sat down and wrote out his progress for the research they wanted him to do for the company. While doing this he received a phone call from the front desk to inform him the garage called and said it would be two weeks before his car would be ready to drive.

After sending the email to his new boss it was not until the next morning that a new car was waiting for him and also letter with complete instruction on how to proceed with his journey. But above all else do not show anybody the diary because it will help us in the long run for finding where all the secrets are located in the world. A thought came to Robert that why should we keep all the secrets from the world and that led him to realize what if it's not the secret bunker or cures they want to keep quiet. It would be that there are people in this world that are hiding in small unseen villages around the area that would no longer benefit to live among us. Now the next steps need to be planned out very carefully because of the new car and strange letter from his boss. Meaning Robert must be careful as to not inform his boss fully about the journey to find the secrets of the world.

In the understanding that being cautious about the company he works for but also for why he is having so many problems with his car and family tragedies. This leads him a full realization about his family blood line and also how the diary could cause harm to everyone in the world. If this happens nobody will be safe from danger because of how people think about certain things when it comes to money and power. The feeling of being watched again showed back up when he checked out of the hotel the next day and while he was driving down the road to the end of his journey. The time has come to pull over and make a call to his mother and to find out if everyone is alright plus no other things has happened in the family. One eerie thing that did happen while talking on the phone with his mother a car that was passing by slowed down enough for him to see who was inside the car. Strangely enough it was nobody he knew but it was strange in itself.

CHAPTER
4

WHILE LOOKING AT THE diary every time he stops and realizes that every line of code has symbols and no letters or numbers in them. But within the symbols gives a clue on which type of languages that it will not be in the diary. In knowing this the clue to which language it might be is the languages that only has symbols in their languages. While thinking very hard about the symbols, Robert did not realize someone had followed him to the diner across the street from the gas station. Robert closed the diary when the waitress came to the table to take his order. As he looked up to see the waitress face a shadow went across the room. After eating he got up to paid for his meal as he was leaving the diner a strange feeling of being watched came over him again. Robert got to his car and started driving down the road again. In doing so the first thought that came to his mind was to never bring out the diary again in public.

The next step in deciphering the diary is to find which languages ancient or modern that only has symbols and nothing else. While doing the research for all the known or unknown languages during the time period for the plague and the secret bunker it only showed a few matches. The internet search only revealed only five select islands that might have this type of symbols without letters for a language. The next step would be to find out which five islands that will match these different codes inside the diary. While doing the research for finding the five islands an email alert came up on his phone. Does anyone know where I stopped at because I only choose this place at the last minute? Robert opened the email and it read; STOP DANGER a knock at your hotel room will happen in 3, 2, and 1. Knock, Knock please answer the door now and say nothing. Signed H.S.S.

Right as soon as the one count hit there was a loud knock at the door, and strangely enough Robert got up to answer the door. When Robert opened the door a messenger was standing in front of him with a large envelope with only his name on the front. Robert looked at the messenger and said, "How can I help you?" The messenger said, "I have a package for Robert Horror and is that you sir?" yes, that is me but I did not order anything. I am only here to deliver this to you and that is all have a good evening sir. The messenger left without a tip or even a goodbye from Robert. When Robert took the package and closed the door and the feeling of being watched disappeared altogether. Walking over to the bed he sat at the edge and thought to himself, how or why is that everything is happening to me and nobody else?

Without opening the strange package Robert went back to work on deciphering the codes in the diary, but a nagging feeling keeps telling him to open the strange package. Before he continued on with the research of decoding the diary Robert moved over to the bed and opened the strange package. Inside the strange and weird package were money and a simple note that says: The money is for a new computer to do your research on because you are being watched by people that are trying to find out our secrets. P.S. Don not tells anyone about this letter or note and please use the money now. Signed H.S.S.

After reading the note it was too late to buy another computer so he will do it in the morning but a phone call came from the front desk. Robert took the phone call and the only thing that was said, "Your computer is ready for pick up now and the price will be $500 dollars and the person on the other end tells Robert the address after which that person hangs up the phone. The last thing that was said please pick up your computer tonight and thank you for shopping with us. Robert hung up the phone and went to his car to go to the address to pick up his computer. Once Robert picked up his new computer and headed back to his hotel room again the feeling of being watched came over him once more but this time it was getting closer than ever.

Robert stepped into his hotel room and noticed something strange all his research and documents were all over the bed and floor of the room. It was a good thing the diary was in his coat pocket and not left in the room while he was gone to get his new computer. After Robert gathered all the documents into one place he turned around and packed up his old computer and placed it into the closet once everything was finished in the room. Afterward Robert opened the box with his new computer and started it u just like any other computer he had in the past, but something about this computer was very different than any other normal computer.

This computer had one added feature and that feature was a hand held scanner attachment connected to it. A single program was on the computer desktop already loaded and programmed into the computer hard drive. Robert scanned the first few pages of the diary and the program slowly worked at deciphering the different codes in the diary. It shows how Hannah was thinking about the different things she sees on a daily basis, but also it shows how smart she was while growing up. By using the dead languages as code that no one would be able to crack the code except for one type of family history.

The program cracked the first entry in the diary which was dated January 1st, 1516. This is first of many entries in the dairy and it speaks of her age which is only 10 years old but strangely it also mention the entrance to the secret bunker is no longer visible from the stream. It also says that her mother caught her in a place where no one must enter unless they are of age. Again the computer program stopped to analyze new data from the symbols but something strange happened every four lines of code equals a full day's activity. Each symbol holds the key to five different words at one time which means within one line of code in the diary can hold fifteen symbols in all. The computer estimated in each line of code it can be a combination of seventy-five words total per line. As the program deciphers each line of code it brings Robert deeper into the world of secrecy. Robert continues to scan the different pages from the diary in turn it took him four hours to scan halfway through Hannah's diary before he started to fall asleep in the chair.

The each line of code is deciphered by the computer program Robert realized that further you got into the diary it starts to talk about her family, the secret bunker and also the different stories of how they all came to be in the area. Only I little bit is written about her family and that is her parents are chemist and she is an only child of her parents. Now it talks about the secret bunker and how it functions. The description of the bunker is as followed and these are the only descriptions available on the bunker in any newspaper articles that was found during the research. The metal that was used to build the bunker was and is a new process of smelting metals together and it is called tenfold process and is hardened steel. The hardened steel is still indestructible because of how the process worked because no records were ever found to show how the process was performed. The corridor that leads to the hidden cryogenics tank is seven foot tall and four foot wide. The corridor is two miles long with air shafts every five feet from the entrance. The entrance into the cryogenics chamber is the size of six feet by two feet. The total room size of the cryogenics chamber is 20,000 square feet by 20,000 square feet. In the center of the room stands a single cryogenic tank, because the surrounding areas next to the walls are full of computers, switches, and other items. When the cryogenic chamber door opened all the lights, computers and even the cryogenic tank came alive.

But before the stories that were written and it says DANGER the alien creature will cause harm to all humans in the world if it is ever let loose upon the world. One of the first stories that Hannah wrote about was how the alien creature blood is very dangerous when it come into contact with human blood and DNA. Two of the unknown viruses are alien in origin, but at the same time, only one virus is dangerous enough to kill everyone in the world. The other unknown virus changes all human DNA sequences genome in the body. The results of the second virus are too dangerous to fully test on any human subjects without proper investigation. As said the first unknown virus is alien in origin because the creature that the virus comes from is alien itself. Plus it can kill everyone in the world, but also the government could be experimenting by transferring blood from the alien creature into other people around the world and nobody would know until it was too late. A scenario for an example would be it starts out with infusing alien blood with the different test subjects but when this happen a lonely lab assistant steals a vial of blood to sale to another research company. That research manufactures the vial of blood into other salable products which it infects the whole world. Mass amount of people dies from the blood products and once the blood is in the people blood stream they can contaminate other people around the world. Now within one year everyone is dead and the world is free to be invaded by an Alien attack force.

The second unknown virus is also alien in origin but this one changes all human DNA into alien DNA. The mutation of human DNA to alien DNA takes three full months to develop in people. During the transformation it makes all humans revert back to their primal stages of evolution. Once the human race has reverted back given what the transformation did to them the world would be back to even before the cave man types were every found in the world. Meaning the human race would be primed to an invasion attack and probably killed by the Alien invasion force. Hence now all of the human race would be killed one way or another which depends on how the world would react towards the invasion.

The daily writing is becoming more important as Hannah is growing older. She starts to talk about learning about becoming a chemist just like her parents. When she turns eighteen years old her advance studies will begin on more complex elements of Earth. Further in the diary it talks about her birthright and also her future skill set that she needs to have in life. Her birthright is to become a Protector of Earth and also ensure the understanding all aspects of chemicals. In understanding chemicals she must study all new species of plants, trees and other things. From the blood line for Protectors of Earth each of them has an understanding that no matter what Earth is always protected. Each generation must learn the ways of secrecy that ensures that nobody remembers them at all in life. Her future responsibilities will be great in learning new ways of protection and chemistry for the purpose of life. Saving life on Earth will become greater than life itself because more danger is on the way.

CHAPTER 5

THE HANDWRITING IN THE diary started to change, but the change is very small due to the way the code was written. Of course, the code starts with the date but now the new person introduced herself as Christina. She goes on to list her skills which include something not expected from these types of people. Besides being a chemist she is also a psychic that has visions of the future. Within the next few pages, she talks about the different visions or dreams that she has been having lately. The writing also changes from a little girl handwriting to a full grown adult with complex wording in each code.

When she turns twelve years old her dreams began to change into visions about the fate and future of the world. Within these visions of Earth, it will show how accurate she was because of all the newspaper articles, books and television programs in the modern age. In the different events will cause the world to plunge into chaos every time they happened. With each event more and more harm will come to the people on Earth. Hell will be unleashed upon the world again because each event will be harmful to the world's population. When Hell is unleashed upon the world again and this time it will be unstoppable. Which means every human life on Earth will be doomed to perish if and when Hell is unleashed upon Earth for a final time before peace comes at a high and steep price. That price would be all of the human race will hang in the balance if caution is not heard in time. This diary serves as a warning to all to prepare for all the events that will doom our planet.

Yes, it is true that most if not all has heard about aliens visiting Earth over the years and into the different decades. As the years goes by the government has interfered with our lives because we are different than the other people in the area. One thing that nobody knows we are the first but we will not be the last people to live in the area of the secret bunker.

Robert slowly realized that some of Christina's predictions have come true already, but now comes the scary part of the diary in the many pages that hold many secrets. First, the secret bunker would be found because of a few blown fuses that had released the cryogenic chamber to the surface. One the cryogenic chamber was released it then turn the alien creature loose upon the world a small town that was built over the secret bunker. The second would be disasters all across the world leaving people homeless and without food to eat. With several disasters happening across the world and they are very dark skies, unexplained deaths, and even murders. Also with some of the disasters happening around the world it will cause the world's population to be decreased by twenty-five percent.

The third is a large meteor striking Earth and causing death to be unleashed again upon the world to do harm to all mankind. When the large meteor strikes the Earth and it will be in the same exact spot as the secret bunker from the past. It will destroy the secret bunker for good and also unleashes the alien creature upon the world again. The final vision that Christina talks about is how some of the Earth population will travel to another planet for war. Even after the Alien Race has come to Earth to start a never-ending war between them and the humans for all resources the planet has to offer them. The vision also tells about a group of humans will use the technology from the alien creature for space travel towards the alien's home world but in doing so the humans will destroy the alien creatures while doing this in the long run.

After reading these few pages of the diary Robert realized that it was too late to heed the warning from all time ago because now the first two stories are true and the third will soon be true enough. The reason for this to fully understand that no matter what we try or even the government tries to meteor will still hit Earth and unleash all hell on Earth before once again peace would be brought to mankind. Within the diary holds the knowledge of power if only we could listen and hopefully understand it all through the eyes of a twelve-year-old girl from the past.

What if the true reason behind the black plague was another explanation for why it had occurred in our world? There are many things in this world we cannot explain because of how they are written or even passed down throughout the ages. The story of the black plague was during the time where no one could give any explanation except for that it was caused because people thought God was angry at them. Too many people, it was a curse that condemned the people in the world for not obeying God's will and commandments, but in truth, it was just one of many things that could not be explained by any common knowledge during that time period. While writing this story I realized there are many explanations for the black plague to occur in the world, but what if instead of rats to be the cause it was an alien that was sent here to cause havoc upon our world. This is my version of the story that may explain the plague, but to only for everyone to understand this story is from my imagination and nothing else.

In the beginning of time, we all are faced with certain choices in our lives because of how we are raised in this world. We are raised with certain beliefs that if any of us did anything wrong or bad a monster would hurt us, but in truth, they are just stories passed down throughout the ages. What if a creature that is unknown to all of us had decided that this world would not benefit us to further understanding and also to use knowledge to better ourselves? This creature is not of this world but an alien sent to destroy our way of life because it deemed us as worthless and unbeneficial to live within our own solar system. It has been said a long time ago there was once a plague upon this world and it was time to destroy it once and for all. This story is also made up of legends, passion, lies, truths and reasons why we must be careful with the wishes we all want in this life or in the next. In our history books in the modern age and with the different research that has been done for the plague, they tell us that the plague came from rats but what is so strange about all of the information is that none of the information tells anything other than where it all started from the beginning. Now one thing to remember is that not all information is told to everyone because of the harm and repercussions for the people that are involved with the information. As we dive into the story of chaos, destruction and even killing the world's population it will lead us to rethink of the different possibilities that we may not be alone in the galaxy. Another question one may ask themselves, are we truly alone or are the government not telling the truth about alien contact?

This time, let us use our imagination to understand what might occur if indeed are ever visited by aliens within our lifetime. Yes, our imagination can run wild even with the smallest part of knowing that we are not alone in the universe. The thought can be helpful only to some if we can just dream of the possibilities of traveling to distant planets in our own lifetime, but to fully understand any of this one might just assume that the technology is just a few years away. What if we already had the technology to travel the distance but are truly worried about how the technology could be used towards the pending doom of Earth. The knowledge may come along soon enough to propel us further into the future with some understanding of space travel, but will it come soon enough to save our world from pending doom. Let's all look at the story that may show us a small glimpse of what would happen if some things were caused by an alien from another world.

The legend begins when a strange and unique plague spread across the world and it would never have been found out that one single thing had caused all the different diseases, viruses plus other causes around the world. As the plague moved across the world certain people started to notice that one person was always in the area when the plague came upon the new victims. As they followed the plague from the starting point to the final ending point, and where it is now called the Lower Rocky Mountains in New Mexico. When the chasers caught up to where the plague is now killing new people on a daily basis, but now it was time to contain the plague to a place no one else will be harmed or killed. After capturing the creature that carried the plague it took some doing to keep it contained while they were building and developing the new process for the cryogenics chamber. It took a full year to develop the process of building the cryogenics chamber with the entrance below the Lower Rocky Mountains.

People have covered up the real reasons why certain diseases and viruses are killing off people and not animals around the world. Even in the new land, there are rumors about certain diseases and viruses came to be that also killed off Native American Indians in the new land. They always blamed the newcomers from a different land that had infected them because of many reasons but the main reason was still unknown to many of them.

In the 16th century, it terrified everyone that people are dying from unknown diseases and viruses that they could not stop. If the whole world knew what was causing the unknown diseases and viruses spreading across they would still be very afraid because no one knew how to stop the diseases and viruses from spreading. They thought it was a curse upon the world when the black plague was spreading all over Europe. Yes, it is true some facts match up with rodents from a ship but to think of any other possibilities would be without an understanding of why this plague came to be in the first place.

Strangely enough certain articles started to appear in Europe that was talking about the true reasons for the plague that had killed millions of people. With the many different understandings for the unknown origin of the plague but in truth the main story that was put out in the articles were the black plague was caused by rats from a ship that had docked in the harbor. But a small side article reads like this and it said the true reasons behind the plague has headed west across the open sea. Even though the plague did not last long but strange things had happened over the years which in turn lead us to the next legend or the next part of the story.

Now this will lead us to the next article that was found in a small town newspaper gazette. Within the next newspaper article it talked about a mysterious cylinder appeared out of nowhere in the middle of the night. But for some reason in this article it reads like the person had first-hand knowledge of everything that had happened in the small town.

CHAPTER

6

A LONG TIME AGO there was a very strange story that had surfaced about a small town in the desert. This news article came from a small town gazette that was twenty miles away from the town that was mention in the article. With mixture of the different articles and the coded diary they both tell the complete story but with added information from the diary. Yes, the articles covered the name of the town, the mysterious cylinder, how the town's people died and also the military cover up story. To understand both the newspaper articles and the coded diary something does not add up to being true and that is something in which is hidden deep within the coded diary. With the short version of the story printed it is now the time to uncover the true full story of what had happened during the time the mysterious cylinder appeared in the area.

The short version is that during the night a mysterious cylinder appeared with a loud booming sound coming from the center of town. Also a strange creature came out from the mysterious cylinder during the night and killed everyone in the small town. While causing havoc all across the small town the mysterious creature looked to be alien in origin but did also look like a wolf that could stand on its own hind legs. It lead to officials calling in reinforcements for help but nobody believed what was truly going on until the doctor of the town called his friend to identify markings that looked like it came from an animal and not a human. Once this happened and the information was sent out to be verified with other professionals in other government offices. Now the town sheriff got a phone call from his own boss and was told that help was coming to stay away from whatever was killing everybody in town. The story goes on to tell that the military showed up and quarantine the whole town and its people because they did not want anything to escape to cause more harm to anyone else. If truth be told the military is only following orders from a higher person from within the government itself. The coded diary goes into further details about what had happened in the town because someone was watching the entire event unfold but that also was not the case for this event.

The youngest daughter of Hannah Smith in which the coded diary was passed down to for reasons that are known only to the Protectors of Earth. The youngest daughter of Hannah Smith and her name is Christina. For many things in this world Christina had predicted that the mysterious cylinder will rise from the ground in the mid 1950's and let the alien creature out to cause havoc within the town itself. Nobody believed her from her own small hidden community because no one had the capability to see the future. Now with the understanding that only one in a million that it is trues a psychic can be born into the world. So now a young child that is to become a Protector of Earth and also a chemist like her parents is fully predicting how things on Earth will eventually harm all of the people in the world. She is predicting when Earth will be in trouble from the alien creature to the far future events of Earth's doom by an alien invasion of Earth.

In the coded diary it showed how the added information of the warning from a child went unheard until it finally happened in front of their very own eyes. As the events unfolded in front of them they realized how important Christina will be to the protection of the human race and also the Earth. With the full understanding of the events the military is covering up the truth behind how the town's people died and were transformed into other alien creatures. The harder the government tried to cover up the details about what happened in the town they did not realize that a few hidden small villages were watching all of the events unfolding in front of them. Meaning even though the government is trying to cover up the true story about the town the people within the few hidden villages are recording the entire events as they were happening in the area.

Once the military and the government got involved with what was happening within the town they had to stop all stories from getting out into the public so they could destroy all evidence of what had happened. So afterward, the military refused to say anything about what happened to the town and people. After town's people died they wanted to ensure nothing got out of the town the military built a fully functional base around the town and also to ensure whatever was killing everyone stayed inside the mysterious cylinder they entombed to mysterious cylinder so it would have one way in and one way out. That was not the strange thing that happened during the story. The strange thing that happened was several years later the military base and the personal with the mysterious cylinder blew up during the night. No survivors were left alive afterward.

But eventually small stories started to leak out about what truly happened to the town and the military base but it was all lies. Meaning the government slowly leaked information about what had happened with the town and the military base in other words they intended to cause no harm in letting people know it was all a hoax. But in truth none of the events ever took place and the town and also the military base was never there in the first place. Over the years different stories of this event surfaced but the true details were never published about what happened on that military base in the desert. The true facts about this very story are covered in a lot of secrets, but strange enough deep somewhere in a top secret file it shows the whole true story. One major fact about this story is the sighting of the mysterious cylinder. This mysterious cylinder is nowhere to be found but a group of people tried to locate the specific spot where the military base was at in the desert.

With each story that tries to explain what was going on but it still does not tell the true understanding of every fact about the story. While the military does a good job covering up the truth, but nobody have all the answers. The government is always covering up stories like this one and says it was nothing but a false story. The false story is slowly becoming true, and here is the real story that was pieced together from different sources.

The Protectors of Earth knows the true story behind what really happened with the town and the military base. In truth the full realization of what could happen even for a period of time that the alien creature can cause havoc among the world. Meaning if there is a small chance of doom for the world's population measures must be put into place to protect everyone on Earth now. With the full knowledge of what happened when it was written in the diary will finally shine the true light upon how dangerous the alien creature would be if left unattended in the world.

While reading both the newspaper articles and the coded diary Robert realized that if this ever gets out that there were hidden villages around the area of the secret bunker that held the alien creature. It would cause uproar within the world because of how the government once again is keeping secrets from the American people. But without conspiracy theories specialists out in the world not all the secrets within the world can truly be hidden from everyone. Knowing this all secret documents, pictures, eyewitness testimony are now in one place that even the president cannot enter into without certain understanding and privileges from the head of the secret organization. That is part of another story for a later date and time.

On the next to the last leg of Robert's journey he realized how important the truth really is about what had happened to the town and the military base. After deciphering more of the coded diary it was fully explained as to why it happened the way it did without anyone truly knowing the full story. With Christina's prediction written down in the diary and now the true story behind the warnings that were placed within the diary for everyone to read. Sadly to say the warnings will never be heard because if they were the world will know the secrets about the hidden villages that surrounds the secret bunker and the alien creature that is hidden inside it. Once the full diary is deciphered everything from the first entry to the last will hold all of the secrets, and when this is realized everyone in the world that has an interest will be seeking the diary in one way or another with that understanding Robert's life will be in danger. With this thought it came to his mind of the car slowing down to see who was in the phone booth but also the feeling while being in the diner across the street from the gas station.

The start of every day is going to be difficult because of the feeling of being watched every time he went outside to get something to eat or even driving down the road. To further complicate things with Robert having the coded diary and driving down the road to where the secret bunker and the alien creature are being held. Within the beliefs of how we react towards other people on a daily basis because with a single action or word towards another person can cause harm to someone. The thought of being watched and followed by people that wants to do harm to the people in the world but also they may want to do harm to the hidden villages and the people within each of them. Another thought came to Robert and that thought was even more horrifying because of the way he felt with everything so far. With this powerful knowledge that this diary had secrets even the world would not want out because they needed to ensure the world is in the dark about all the secrets of the world.

The legend or stories from all those years ago can come back to haunt anyone because even for them they did not heed the warnings for protecting the world from harm. We are faced with difficult choices in our lives that lead each of us down a path that nobody can come back from and due to the knowledge that anyone can hold it against us. Meaning if we do not protect ourselves from harm due to the other worldly aliens. The government has always said there are no aliens from another world that has ever visited us from some long away distant planet. This secret has been hidden away even from the people that saw an unidentified object falling from the sky that looked to be an alien spacecraft. Even with witnesses saying they saw something that was unexplainable to be explained in simple terms like it was a weather balloon that fell from the sky. The government has always tried to cover up known stories about visiting aliens from other worlds, but also it shows how with this information that has been coded into the diary is for the good of the world. So not the choice is ours to make should we continue to believe in aliens or that there is no life on other worlds. Now for the legend and the story behind the events about what happened with the mysterious cylinder and saving the world.

CHAPTER 7

ON A CLEAR DARK night with the stars shining in the sky a very loud noise came from the center of town. A single lone man walked towards the loud noise and found something in the very center of town. The strange item the lone man saw was a seven-foot tall cylinder standing upright. The lone man walked around the seven-foot tall cylinder and noticed that it had no door. He went to touch the cylinder and it felt cold, but the strange part of it all. It had no markings anywhere on the outside of the cylinder. Slowly the other people of the small town started to come towards the center of town. Everybody was afraid of the mysterious cylinder except the lone man that first saw the cylinder.

The only police officer finally showed up and told everybody to stand back and not touch it. The lone man said, "Too late I already touch it and nothing happened." The police officer looked at him and said, "Go to my office and wait there for me. Do you understand?" The lone man said, "What for I did nothing wrong?" The police officer said, "Just do it and now!" The lone man said, "Yes, Sir."

As the lone man was walking off the police officer asked for rope and stakes to rope off the mysterious cylinder so nobody will touch it.

After 20 minutes had passed he went back to his office to talk some more to the man that found the cylinder, and also to call for some help. First, the police officer called for help but nobody would believe him about was in the center of town. Secondly, he turned to the man that found the cylinder and asked, "Why did you not call for help when you found the mysterious cylinder?" The man said, "I was more curious about what it was than calling for help. Plus I know that I was not the only one that heard the noise when the mysterious cylinder got here. Now was I sir?" The police officer said, "Yes, that is true but still you should have called for help."

The main question is since nobody believes you about the mysterious cylinder, "What should we do about it?" The police officer said, "We do nothing about it until someone comes to check on us." The man said, "When will that be sir?" The police office said, "In two weeks, and that is when my boss comes by to check on everything in the area."

From this point on everyone should go about their daily routine and not worry about the mysterious cylinder in the center of town. Do you understand me? The man said, "Yes, I do understand, but what about those people that will not obey the law?" The police officer said, "They will be dealt with in due time."

During the night, the man that touched the mysterious cylinder awoke with a frightful nightmare. In the nightmare, it showed that everyone in town was dead, but the strange thing was it was like nothing anybody had seen before in their lifetime. The next morning people awoke to do their daily activity but they had noticed something different. The owner of the bakery, stables, and a couple of other places where not open yet. The group of people at the bakery started to look around the bakery for the owner but found blood instead. Someone ran to the police officer and told them that they found blood at the bakery.

The police officer ran to the bakery to see what was going on. Once he got there the blood lead him straight to the back of the bakery, but there was nobody anywhere around the bakery. All of a sudden a woman scream came from the stables and the police officer ran towards the screams. Once the police arrived he noticed more blood all over the place, but again nobody anywhere. He sent everybody home and told them not to tell anybody what has happened here today and also to stay home until they were told otherwise. He went to go get the man from yesterday and ask him for help. When the police officer arrived at the man home he had noticed that blood was all around on the porch. He went in to see if the man was alright but nobody was home. He searches all over the home but once he went into the barn there was the man in a pool of blood. He could not figure out if it was the man's blood or someone or something else's blood. The police officer finally got him to his truck and took the man to the doctor's office to see what was wrong. The doctor exam the man and found something strange the man had a single scar on his back from the neck down to his butt.

The doctor and the police officer left the room to talk about what needs to be done. The doctor said, "He needs to be taken care of and you need to go find whatever did this to man and fast." The police officer explains what else he found in town also and asked the doctor, "What should I do next? If my own boss does not, believe me, who else should I call about the events that unfolded here in town?" The doctor said, "I will talk with them and explain what is going on. Now go and search the whole town for everyone that has disappeared and to see if there is any more blood around town."

After the police officer left he went back to the man on the table and searched him again. This time, he found something that did not belong, and it was something that felt like bone but it was not bone. The item was metal shaped to look like a bone. The doctor has to wait until the man wakes up and ask what happened to him during the night.

The police officer spent most of the day searching the town and found ten people disappeared during the night, and nothing but blood was left behind. He said, "It is the time that I called my boss again and explain everything to him. When he arrived back at his office instead of him calling his boss the opposite happened. His boss called and asked him, "What is going on down there? You called yesterday and made no sense and now the doctor called me and said that I needed to come down there right now." Sir, I have something to tell you during the night something happened that it will be hard to understand unless you see it for yourself. His boss said, "I am leaving now and will be there tonight." The police officer said, "Thank you sir and I will be waiting for you."

At eight o' clock that night, the police officer boss showed up to his office and demanded to see what was going on. The police officer took his boss to all of the bloody sites and then to the man that found the mysterious cylinder at the doctor office. His boss said, "Why is he still here he seems to be doing fine now?" The police officer told the doctor to turn him over and show him the man back. As the doctor turn the man over the police officer boss saw the scar from the neck to his butt. His boss said, "I need to see the cylinder now!" Ten minutes later they were at the mysterious cylinder and his boss asked, "Did anyone touch the cylinder?" The police officer said, "Yes, the man at the doctor's office."

His boss left to make a special phone call and then came and said, "The right people for this will be here in the morning to find out what is going on here." The police officer said, "Yes, Sir." They both stayed up and watched from the window to see if anything happened during the night. Something strange happened, the cylinder opened and a creature came out of it on two legs. The creature looked around and ran around town and right before dawn went back into the cylinder again.

The next morning both the police officer and his boss went to the cylinder and saw nothing no doors or handles. They both heard screams coming from multiple places again. They ran to see and there was blood everywhere they looked and realized that ten more people disappeared during the night. Two hours later the military showed up and put up a perimeter fence around the town. They set up a command base outside of town and called the police office to see what has happened before they got there.

The police officer answered the phone and then handed it to his boss. His boss talked with the man on the other end and explained what is going on. The man on the other end hung up the phone and turned toward his boss and said, "It is confirmed hostile in town and 20 people missing and one in the doctor's office injured. I suggest max level perimeter and nothing gets out alive except for us." The general said, "Are we sure about what is going on?" The army solider said, "Yes,

Sir!" The general said, "Do it and let me know when it is done." The soldier said, "Yes, Sir."

In a matter of a few short hours, the town was surrounded with max level perimeter and guards towers. A crew of five people in radiation suits walked into town to look at the mysterious cylinder and the injured man at the doctor's office. There were no readings at the mysterious cylinder in or around the area. Then they went to the doctor's office to see the injured man and noticed that he was still lying down on an exam table. The man was awake but not able to talk to anyone, and they looked at his back and decided to leave with him in tow. They told the doctor that he would be looked after outside in isolation until he is well enough to travel. It was time to go back to the command center and figure out what do to next.

Once they got back to the command center they put the injured man into the isolation room and started running multiple tests on him to see what was going on in his body. Each test they did just seemed to show that in different parts of his body was turning into metal. The strange thing was his body outside looked normal. It was like his was turning into a mechanical robot from the inside out. It was time to see what really was on the inside of his body and to see if he was in danger. The man was being scanned once an hour to see if anything changes. When nightfall came the man body started changing again, but this time, more of his organs changed to mechanical parts. They also noticed that when nightfall came the creature from inside the mysterious cylinder came out and ran everywhere in town. This time, it stopped by the perimeter fence and stood up to see what was going on. Next, the creature went to the doctor's office and noticed the injured man has vanished. After that, the creature killed more than ten people it killed 20 people instead. After that, the creature went back into the cylinder to get ready for the next nightfall.

The next morning the police officer and his boss searched the town and found more blood everywhere. They called the command center to inform them about more people disappeared, and they said yes we know. The doctor's watching the injured man looked at his scans and noticed 20 more bones had turned into metal bones during the night.

CHAPTER

8

THE GENERAL REALIZED EVERY time the creature kills a bone in the injured man turns into metal. It was time to do something about the creature and the mysterious cylinder. If they do not everyone in town will be killed and the injured man will be all metal and too powerful to be stopped. The general called to get the OK to destroy and bring back the injured man to be studied. The hostile is aggressive and will not stop until the full population is killed. Two hours later the general received the authorization to destroy the town and the hostile. One hour later all military personnel left the area and the injured man was transported back to the main base for studying. Thirty minutes later the air strike team arrived and dropped a massive amount of bombs on top of the cylinder and the town. When the fire and dust cleared the town was gone but the mysterious cylinder was still there in one piece. The military decided to build a base around the mysterious cylinder so nobody would find it. They also put a 30-foot wall around the cylinder to protect everyone on the new base from the creature.

One hour after the town and everybody was destroyed the doctor's scanned and x-rayed the injured man and realized that all of his bones are now made of metal. The injured man broke free from the straps holding him down on the table. He got up and stood for a few minutes to get his bearings. Once that was done he moved toward the door and found the door locked. He stopped and looked at the door and pulled on the handle with all of his might, and the door came off the hinges and door frame in one pull. The alarms rang out loud to announce the injured man has left the room. The injured man walked until he meets multiple guards in his way, but when the guards told him to stop he did not listen and said, "I am leaving to go home." The guards repeated, "Stop or we will shoot you dead!"

The injured man continued walking and the guards opened fired on the injured man, but, strangely enough, he kept on walking as the bullets hit him all over his body. He looked down and noticed that he was bleeding but nothing was stopping him from walking away. He kept walking and the guards attacked him with knives plus any other hand to hand combat weapons skills. Each guard fell to the ground dead as the injured man moved down the hall. It was like the injured man had no way of dying. Finally, the injured man got to the closest exit and opens the door. The sunlight hit his face and it felt great to be outside and free. The next thing he knew military men was surrounding him with all types of weapons that would cause death in every which a way possible for a human being. It was time to leave this place or find where the mysterious cylinder is and complete the process of transforming into a complete creature for this new world.

With each step, the injured man took more and more soldiers died there was only one way out of the base and that is through the main gates that are being guarded be massive tanks and weapons. It was time for the injured man to understand his full potential of his new body. He thought of something strange and before he could stop himself he had changed into a four-legged animal. This animal was no ordinary animal it was a metal cat that was faster than any known animal on earth. He started running towards the front gates and realized besides being fast he could jump high into the air and attack anyone that tries to stop him.

Twenty minutes later he was at the front gates and transformed back into a human being. This time, he needed to figure a way out without hurting himself, and then he realized no matter what he did, he could not hurt himself in any way possible. It was time to find where the mysterious cylinder went to and return to it. It was like the cylinder was guiding him towards it. It was time to stop playing and leave now before they could stop him. He destroyed half the gates and then turned back into an animal and took off towards his hometown. Three hours later he arrived back at his home area and realized something different about the place. A military base is now where the town use to be, but he senses the cylinder in the middle of the base under heavy guard. What other things can he turn into in his new body? He started thinking again and this time, it was a huge ground hog to dig his way towards the cylinder under the ground.

After three hours he was almost to the cylinder, but he felt something strange as he is getting closer. The closer he got the stronger he felt and bigger he got in size. When it was time to go up to the surface he noticed that the area around the cylinder was as small as they could build around the cylinder. He fixed that and broke through the wall wide enough to transform back into a human. He put his hands on the cylinder and it opened to let him inside, but once inside it was huge. The creature came out of the shadow and meets the human that became the creature creation. They both stared at each other and started talking in a strange language, not of this world.

It seemed that the creature and the human being are part of a whole being because the creature was it, brother or sister. It seemed that every time they thought of something in their heads they changed into a few seconds afterward. It was time to complete the process so they could complete their mission and return home. It was time to change the human race into what they should have been before the dawn of time. It was time for the humans to evolve from the flesh form and change into what they truly are and that is a massive invasion army for the Martians. The creature was once in charge of a massive army on mars but the Martians rebelled back and destroyed their planet.

This time, the creature will create the perfect army to conquer the galaxy. With each person that is changed into their real form, it was one step closer to perfection. The creature proclaimed he was God of all races and planets of the galaxies. He sent out his new creation and called him Alpha to change the human race. Alpha obeyed and the first order of business was to destroy all military personnel on the base. The first day Alpha changed half of the military personnel and sent them to his creator. All of the top military personnel were changed also so they could send Alpha into other places around the United States. It took several weeks before the rest of the military based changed into their evolved race. This time, an order was set among the newly evolved race and Alpha was in charge of the whole process.

It was time to move on to other locations to spread the new race among the dying human race on earth. This time, it was the newly evolved creatures that were disguised as military personnel that were sent to other bases while Alpha accompanied the general of the base to the Army headquarters in Washington D.C. As the general was introducing Alpha to everybody he slowly remembered every face and person of high ranking level in the place. It will soon be time to take over this place and declare war on everybody else that will not follow the creator. Alpha decided that time was needed to evolve all of the people in this place. The process started slowly by moving around the newly evolved personnel to certain place in the United States. Then each of the evolved personnel received updated information and then started the process of changing all of the personnel in the different places. It took a full year to evolve every last person in the United States.

Other countries started to notice a change in the way the United States was conducting business, but it was too late each of the major ethnic races was changed and sent back to their home country of origin. It took another five earth years to change 99 percent of the world's population to the evolved Martian race. The one percent that is left will all be destroyed in due time, but the only way for everybody to try to change back to normal to kill the creator and Alpha. If they can find them at all in this new world they have created.

Where are they in the new world? With the new creation of a Martian race can it be known that this planet is doomed just like the real Martian home world? The one percent has a plan that will depend on new technology in destroying the evolved race. This new technology has to be stolen from the creator himself, but how will that happen? The only way near them would mean they too would be changed into the evolved Martian race. The evolved Martian race can tell the difference between human and the evolved Martian race. It was time to see what weapons could be made to make a difference between survival and death.

The one percent of the world population began to gather in one place that is underground and unknown to anyone in the world. The only place that is unknown to the rest of the world is a new underground base that was being built during the cold war. Every resource to be known to mankind was in the newly built underground base. They formed a chain of command for the new army to save mankind from the threat to the human race. This time, they set up ways of detecting the evolved race before they entered into the new base. They had to develop new technology to detect the type of metal that is being used in the evolved Martian race.

It was noticed that each new evolved Martian was not fully programmed until they meet Alpha or the creator. Just before the newly evolved Martian changed fully they were confused and did not know what to do until it was told. That is when it was time capture the newly evolved Martian and run any test to see what could kill them or change them back to normal. It took multiple tries and finally they could stop the signal from being transmitted to Alpha or the creator. Once the transmission was stopped it looked as if the person was dead, but really it was waiting for the signal to be turned back on to receive instructions again.

It was time to see what type of metal that the bones are being turned into while the creature is transforming. Two people operated on the transformed creature and found that every bone in the creature body was connected in every way just like a normal human. The strange thing was the organs were slowly being changed to convert them towards the metal body. They took out every metal bones and organs from the creature body to study each of them closer so they can deal the max damage when it comes time to either change them back or to destroy each of them. With every step of the new technology and the studying of the creatures, they can find a way around the security problem which is getting close enough to the creator or Alpha to kill them dead.

CHAPTER
9

NOW IS THE TIME to create weapons to kill or neutralize these creatures. With every step of new technology, the truth comes out on how different people invent things. It is time to find every last survivor in the world so it will be possible to mount a full attack on the creator base of operations. Once all of the proper steps have been taken then it will be time to attack the Alpha and the creator, but until then it is time to produce a fully functioning type of weapon, armor, and vehicles that will be needed for the attack.

It takes another six months until all of the remaining survivors are found and another two months to gather every component to make the new items for the war. With each convoy and also with each attack on the different cities that leads to where the Alpha and the creator the rebels are getting closer. It is like a new world war has begun and this time, it will be for the freedom for the whole entire world. With each passing day more of the surviving human race dies, but then the enemy also dies. Soon the time will tell if anyone will be able to survive this war.

Six weeks has passed and they are half way to the creator main area, but something has changed with each one of them, because they are getting stronger. Each creature they face it seems that each one knows what is happening to them before the soldiers knew what they were going to do during the battle. As the attack force reaches each city they have to use different tactics to confuse the enemy. It took another two months before the rebels surrounded the main city where the Alpha and the creator are living.

It took another week before the full city was surrounded by the rebels. It was time to mount an attack that will end all wars in the world forever. The rebels will cause several distractions around the city while an elite force will confront the Alpha and also the creator for one last time. At dawn, the attack started on schedule and the main elite force moved towards the center of the city. Once they arrived they used one of the lesser creatures to open the cylinder so they may enter without detection. Once the elite force enters the cylinder it became all too clear that they should have brought more people with them. It was too late the cylinder door closed behind them and they were trapped. They continued forward towards the signal of hopefully either Alpha or the creator. It is time to take out the guards that were surrounding the main chamber and they enter into the main chamber.

The creator became aware that someone had entered into the main chamber, but strangely no alarms went off to announce anyone was present. The closer the elite force got and the worse the feeling of death surrounded them all. Alpha was standing between the elite force and the creator for protection. It was time to change ammo and weapons to finish this war for good. They fired at the creator and struck Alpha instead, but the strange thing that had happened was when Alpha was hit the creator bleed instead. So the elite force fired upon both the Alpha and also the creator at the same time and nothing happened to either one of them. They decide to kill the creator first and then confront Alpha afterward. After multiple shots to Alpha and the creator went down and bleeds out but while doing so the blood from the creator went towards Alpha and made him even stronger than before. Once the last bullet struck the creator and then Alpha grew in size plus in strength and started attacking the elite force one by one. The very last elite force member had instruction to blow up the inside of the mysterious cylinder and leave no trace behind for unknown reasons. It was time to wait for the creatures to change back to normal, but they did not because they stayed the same. After the last elite force member was left he had no choice and to use a bomb to blow up the creator and Alpha together. When the bomb went off nobody was injured in the blast. How is that possible no one or nothing should have survived the huge blast?

What if there is no other way to stop this invasion but to blow up the world itself. In the end after the blast it was all up to the small army to kill every last enemy without killing the creator and also the Alpha. This time, the rebels are taking the fight to the enemy and will not stop until every last one is dead. The rebel forces are starting to think that whatever they do; they will not win this war. Now is the time to fight for survival and to kill every last enemy that wants to destroy the human race. This world needs to turn into a vast military fighting force to destroy every single threat. This threat is real as it comes for the human race and it is time to upgrade all the weapons and vehicles for the advanced final attack against all of the alien creatures.

As the battle wages on more and more people on both sides are dying as the creator and Alpha grows in strength. The only way to stop this war is to ensure the creator and Alpha stays inside the mysterious cylinder. For reasons behind this is clear when both of them are locked away all other creatures can be taken care of during the final battles. The only way to ensure both of them can no longer harm anyone outside in the world.

As all of this is happening in front of the hidden village that that was hidden in the forest that still had some Protectors of Earth inside. When the village finally saw what was happening to the area and also to the people they acted upon their teachings. Now comes the part of the story that nobody believes in because of how it was written in the article. The next part is like something from a magician show and from some strange weird other planet thing. A single Protector of Earth person from the hidden village walked out of the forest and went straight towards the mysterious cylinder. It seems as if the lonely person was invisible to all of the alien creatures it encountered on the way to the mysterious cylinder. Without using any lesser alien creature that person touched the mysterious cylinder and just walked in like it was normal.

The next part was seen from the outside of the mysterious cylinder. While watching everything that was going on outside of the mysterious cylinder and then all lesser alien creatures stops by standing in place. In another ten minutes the mysterious cylinder moved back under the ground to never be seen again. Strangely enough all lesser alien creatures that were still alive reverted back to their normal human being selves without any side effects. When the reports started coming in from different places around the area that the lesser alien creatures are changing back to normal human people. Within a matter of a few days the lesser alien creatures that were left alive all changed back to normal. In doing so they had no memory of what had happened to them or even to the world.

From that moment on the world had no clue about what had happened to them, but the few that were left from the rebel army did not tell or say anything about the world. In doing so only a select few were chosen to join the Protectors of Earth. While all of this is happening all records that has ever been made will be erased totally and completely for the one's that does want to join them. Also to ensure all records are destroyed they will have a choice to be dead when people are found around the area of the attack.

In the understanding with everything around the world in what has happened to them but it shines a huge light on how life can be for anyone. The knowledge one might have in this world is only a small amount compared to the vast amount of knowledge one has if they lived on every single planet that may or may not hold life. Meaning the different planets that are known or even unknown to people across the vast galaxies in the different universes can hold information to help the human race. The vast knowledge that not any one person holds, but having multiple people holding the complete knowledge is understandable for protecting the human race from harm. The time has grown short because the world needs to be further along when dealing with any new technologies that still needs to be developed for future events that would destroy Earth for one final time.

The time table has been moved up sooner than the Protectors of Earth would like it to be because of how the world's population was reduced by thirty percent in all. In knowing this it is time to enact protocol five. Protocol five is the complete jump in technology from level one to level ten which means it is time to advance all technology around the world. It in turns the world into a complete intertwined connect world that any Protector of Earth that can send any warning to anyone when trouble arises. If trouble arises by another invasion or attack from the creature in the mysterious cylinder an alert will go out to notify everyone that danger is here. This is to ensure the safety for all humans on Earth from now on because they are our future.

Yes, it is true that Earth is very far from where they need to be in protecting themselves from harm. With the knowledge that is learned by watching and interacting with the human race one may think that they will never be ready to encounter aliens from other planets. The time has come for the Protectors of Earth to ensure every aspects of protection are put in place for when the next even will occur. As the world continues to move along at the pace it is traveling no one is safe from harm even if it is from their own people here on Earth. Now is the time for all of humanity to join together in protector each other from harm, because they are still dealing with petty things like race wars, gun violence, murders, crime of passions and even ritualistic killings for many things. This will still make Earth very weak when the time comes to protect the Earth from harm. In knowing this it is up to the hidden villages around the secret bunker to keep a watchful eye on the world's population plus the people of Earth.

One last thing to remember majority of us think we are alone in this vast expansion of our universe but to truly tell everyone this is not so will take a major toll on everyone ego. Meaning our universe is only one of millions, billions or even trillions of universes out there that we have not been able to discover yet. So now is the time to think ahead and safeguard our lives as if it is the only one we got to live. Only one being knows all and sees all. God is the Alpha and Omega, Beginning and the End but also the First and the Last to know everything that is happening to us as humans. The knowledge that we may be alone in the vast galaxies and universes is the biggest mistake we could even make even for ourselves.

CHAPTER
10

AFTER A LONG BATTLE with the Alpha and the creator which also includes all of the lesser alien creatures. During the long battle in which caused a lot of destruction and chaos for the whole area but strange enough the hidden villages were not damaged at all. Since the creator did create the Alpha creature to do his dirty business which included collecting all of the lesser alien creatures for destroying mankind all over the world. It turns out that the creator is indeed the same alien creature that was in the bunker from all that time ago. Strange enough when the mysterious cylinder appeared in the middle of town it was just an exit that was created when the bunker was first built in 1515. When the bunker was first built in 1515 there was supposed to be one way in and one way out but the builders failed to notify everyone involved with the construction on the bunker. No one realized at the time that the builders installed an exit for people to leave without being noticed, and it just so happened the reason for the mysterious cylinder to appear was a pressure switch was deactivated because of fuses being blown. With an added effect of the fuses being blown it caused a great fear with the town's people that had heard the noise during the night. When certain fuses were blown it had caused the mysterious cylinder to be released and it was sent to the surface. When the mysterious cylinder was sent to the surface it released the alien creature into the world again.

With the knowledge from the Protectors of Earth the people that did survive had to go into hiding for reasons that were not just beyond their imagination but it was to safeguard them from further harm when the real invasion is to occur. In the understanding of how things work in the world it comes with the utmost knowledge that is needed to further protect the human race from themselves because of all the world wars, murders, gun violence and other violent actions against all other humans on Earth. Each of us holds the true meaning of life in our hands but what is truly not understood by some people is that their actions can lead someone to harm other innocent people in the world. Robert further realized when deciphering the diary it just not held coded warning for the pending doom but it also held the full knowledge of how to stop the alien creature attack force from causing harm to any humans in the world.

In the diary besides warning and pending doom on almost every page it also included on how to defeat the invading alien creature force with maximum amount force done to them and not to harm any humans in the process. One added bonus with the diary in Robert's hands is that the safety for him and family is necessary at all cost because of how dangerous the information is in the hands of people that wants to rule the whole world with disregard for human life. It has been a long time in the making but our world has been controlled by forces from within even though people do not want to admit it is true. Our world is being pulled in multiple directions because of how the different governments wants to control the world but in truth the world is being pulled by a much greater force to the unseen eye in the world. Too bad that the world has no clue in which direction the world is being pulled due to the understanding of how things truly work.

The people that live in the hidden villages around the secret bunker sends out certain people with a certain skill set that can be included into the working class within the world. With the knowledge and full understanding of how the world direction that it needs to go in it is now up the Protectors of Earth to ensure they advance towards preparing the world for an alien attack force. The world has always been able to cover up somethings in the newspapers, radio stations or even on televisions because of how things may look in the news. Yes, it is true that other stories replace the real ones but that is because of how the different governments work in our world. Their military has always covered up certain stories or news articles about mysteries that could not be explained with some true facts about what happened. This time, the government said, "There has never been any town called by that name and all the strange stories that have been spread across the world are just rumors." Within the next few weeks, the government had erased all known information about the town and its history from any books, articles or even the knowledge of the people that did survive the attack that did within the town. Yes, it is true that any government is capable of covering up any story or events but they cannot cover up the truth from the people that did live in the town at the town.

It has come to Robert's attention that he is being watched again but this time it is different because as he was driving down the road heading towards New Mexico the same car has been behind him for three hours now. As Robert pulls off the road to get gas, food or even to relax for a little bit the same car that is following him does the same thing. As Robert enters into the diner to eat and siting in the farthest booth from the door but what he sees is shocking because of whom he sees entering into the diner. Strangely enough the person that who enters into the diner after he does looks strangely like his father but that cannot be because when he called his parents on the last pit stop and his father was at home in New York. That was not the strange part of the whole entire event at the diner because the man that looked like his father came and sat down at Robert's table without even asking to sit down. They both stared at each other and no one said anything to each other for over five minutes. The reason for this is because of how this person looks like Robert's father but knowing it is not gave Robert eerie thoughts of his own when the man in front of him spoke.

When the man spoke he said only a few words before he got up to leave the diner altogether and those words were, "Do not continue on your journey or you will die." Once these words were spoken the man got up and left plus never turned around to see if he was being followed out of the diner by Robert. For reasons unknown Robert did not even leave his seat when the unknown man just got up and left without saying anything else to anyone in the diner. As Robert is eating his meal in the diner the diary that is in his coat pocket felt like it was getting heavier and heavier as the minutes ticks by but once Robert got into his car something happened. A car came out of nowhere and went right through the diner and ended up in the booth that he was sitting in just moments ago.

How strange was that to occur just moments after he left the diner or was that supposed to happen before he left the diner to ensure that he never finished his journey. Again getting back into his car and taking off to finish his journey which ends in New Mexico but also it is getting to the point that every time he stops something strange always happen to him or his car. After stopping just three hours out of where all the stories were being written about in the diary and also the newspaper articles. After stopping for the last night of his journey and when he checked into his room another mysterious package was waiting from him but the funny thing was even he did not know that he was stopping here at this hotel for the night.

The package held the final key to everything in the coded diary and also in the world for things are about to come to a full stop on a world that has spun around for eons. Once the final steps are taken the world will never be the same afterward, but also it will hurl Earth towards a solution that has never seem possible until the next event occurs in the world. Yes, during the early stages of space exploration and trying to understand what is out there in space but this is different. There was discovery that was not fully understood until the mid-21st century. The people that were studying the stars and planets saw something in the big bright night sky, and what they found could not be believed until it was confirmed by the government with a bigger telescope. The closer the object got and the easier for the other people around the world could see what the object was in the far distance. The mysterious object was a large type meteor heading straight for Earth. The only part that is not understood is when the large size meteor going to hit the Earth.

After the diary was fully deciphered and the package was opened and both was put side by side it showed and spelled out what was to occur within the next few days. Meaning Robert finally turned on the television set to see what was on and realized the news anchor had interrupted to broadcast a news report. That news report was talking about a large size meteor was heading towards Earth and the impact will be the lower mountain range in New Mexico. A strange thought occurred to Robert during the last pit stop on his journey. The thought was if I reach to the city where the secret bunker and all of the hidden villages are what will happen once I enter into the area. Which means the impact site is the same site as both of the secret bunker and the hidden villages that houses the Protectors of Earth.

With the full knowledge of the deciphered diary and the items in the mysterious package it will be Hell on Earth once more when both of them items are combined once and for all. Meaning the deciphered diary and the items from the mysterious package holds the key to finding the Protectors of Earth main elder plus the protection item that is needed to ensure safe passage into the hidden village where the elder lives. As the events that are about to unfold as the large size meteor heading towards Earth will reveal the true understanding of what will happen to everyone on Earth during this event. The eyes within the world will be opened fully to the events of the world which means all who are involved of covering up all past actions will soon be uncovered for the world to see in the full bright shining light. After the meteor hitting Earth which kills almost everyone in the impact zone will have to survive one other disaster that is hiding under the surface.

CHAPTER
11

ONE DAY OVER THE news, a news anchor reported that something was wrong at the White House and no one is supposed to be talking to anyone right now. That day in the afternoon, there was supposed to be a speech from one of the president's advisors but the speech was canceled at the last minute due to some error in the speech. For the next six weeks, there had been no news coming from the White House because people were running around all nervous and scared about saying something wrong to the press. It was all due to last minute information that has changed in the speech and now the speech had been changed to include extra information. Over a week has passed and still nothing has been spoken about the speech until one day, a statement came from the White House about what is going on during the last six weeks or more. The statement said, "A scientist has discovered a large meteor that has broken away from the asteroid field near the Milky Way and is approaching earth at a high rate of speed. Also, the large meteor's gravity has attracted other small meteors along its path.," said someone from the White House.

For the next six months, the government has been announcing that there is no meteor heading towards earth. They have been saying all this time it was all a hoax by someone in the White House and that person has been dealt with in a reasonable manner. As the days turned into weeks and the weeks turned into months everyone went about their business like usual, as they always did in the past. Everyone went to work as they normally did every day and went home as normal as if nothing has ever happened at all for the past two months. The reason being is that the government has been telling everyone there was no meteors' coming towards us at all. By the end of the same week, the White House finally came forth to tell people "there was something wrong and it will be revealed soon enough. The reason being is that we were not sure about the information that we had in our files, but sure enough the information was correct and that is why we are telling you now. Also, that is the reason why we have changed our attitude about the meteors that are approaching earth's orbit."

When the White House finally had a press conference about the meteors that are heading towards us but this is just a preliminary announcement to tell people what we have discovered at a later time. This is because we are not fully sure of how far away the meteors are the scientist having discovered something about the meteors and we have to make sure that we are correct before we tell you the public so we don't scare anyone into a panic." The only way that the government will tell the people is through tiny news stories throughout the world. The channels all across the world will tune into the president's speech about the meteors that are coming towards earth. When the time comes, the president will have to tell everyone what the government is doing to stop the meteors. The President of the United States came on television to tell everyone "there are meteors heading towards earth but there is nothing we can do to stop them. When we discovered the meteors that are heading towards earth, we tried different ways to stop them but nothing worked. We tried nuclear warheads, bombs, and even our most powerful laser that we have in outer space. While the meteors are traveling through outer space, they are gaining momentum. The momentum of the meteors are going faster than we ever seen and expected before. We tried to figure out the size and weight of each meteor that is approaching earth's orbit, but it took two long weeks to finally figure out the size and weight and the shape of each meteor. While the meteors travel through the earth's atmosphere small chunks from each of the meteors will fall off to reduce the size and weight and the shape of each of the meteors. As the meteors pass through the atmosphere at a high rate of speed they break up into smaller pieces, and the ones that do make it through the atmosphere will still be big enough to cause damage. They would destroy houses, cars buildings and many other things. No matter if, they are sitting still or even moving at a high rate of speed.

Now let us talk about the largest meteor of them all. The meteor that we are talking about is so enormous that we are calling it a global killer. The size of the meteor is big as the state of California and the weight of the meteor is about 2,000 metric tons before it goes through the earth's atmosphere. Once through the atmosphere the size and weight of the meteor is reduced to about 1,500 metric tons or maybe less if we hope. Its size is that of a two-story house with a garage, but the shape of the meteor looks like it is long and oval. After all of the chunks that fall off from the big meteor, it is still big enough to cause damage to the ground. When the main meteor hits the ground it causes a massive shock-wave through the earth crust so far that the entire area will be flattened, all throughout the city except for the outer east part of the city."

Therefore, for the last six months the government has been talking about the enormous meteor that is heading towards earth. We are not sure of when it will hit earth's atmosphere because when we estimated the time and distance of the meteors they were going fast but now the momentum of the meteors has slowed down but they are still on their way here. After all this time it finally came that the government gave a tape to each of the news station to show on the event of the meteors approaching earth's orbit. Finally, on a day that no one suspected the newscast of a particular massage that will be sent over the airwaves to everyone's home, computers, and cell phones that the end was coming soon for the citizens on earth. The message came from someone that is not authorized to send that message out and that person has been found and dealt with in a proper manner. The real message was sent out by the government to be played the moment the meteor is close enough to see. Sunday night the message stopped showing on all of the channels around the world at midnight. From midnight on every channel had nothing but static on them. After the airing of the message, no one could sleep a wink that night. Should they fear the meteor or should they fear that this is not really happening to them. Another question they should be asking themselves is "should they go to work or should they stay home that day?"

When the early morning came, some of the people wanted to stay home and other people felt they should go to work. Five in the morning the message came across the television sets again, but this time the message has not changed at all. The message was still playing on television in people homes all across the world. It started showing the same message again as they have for the last few weeks. When the clock struck six the message stopped playing and a person came onto the television and started saying some things about what will be happening later on today. "Please everyone that can hear this broadcast listen to me very carefully to what I have to say. I am here to tell you that everything will be alright and that you need to go back to work as nothing ever happened in the past few weeks," said the newscaster. Everyone that was up and eating at the time or was getting dressed for work heard the newscast and thought to themselves, "that something was strange about the way that the newscaster said everything this morning." When people all around the world thought to themselves, "Is why all of a sudden we should act like nothing has happened in the past few weeks of our lives?"

All day Monday, the news has been the same telling everyone to go back to work and the ones that did not go called in sick, which were many people around the world. By midday the people that went to work noticed that the traffic was easier to travel because there was not many vehicles on the road today like their usually is on any other day. At five o'clock in the evening, everyone was getting off from work and the drive hoke was like driving through the countryside.

On Tuesday morning, it was like any other morning during the week it was slow and dragging until the weekend comes. Everyone was getting up and ready for work so they would not be late. They turned on the television so they could watch the news to see if anything else is going to happen today. There is nothing new today on the news so everyone left to go to work before they are late. Everyone started showing up for work around eight thirty in the morning like they always did every morning like clockwork if they didn't call in sick. The parking lot was about half-full at eight thirty that morning.

Now let us speak about the office building that this event takes place at; it is four stories high and a half block long. The first floor of this building is full of glass windows, and a set of glass doors, which enchants the building from a far. There are columns that reach up to the second floor of the building, and the rest of the building stands tall and proud to be a part of the same building.

Almost nine o'clock in the morning the sky turned black as if it time for a solar eclipse. When the sky turned black, a noise was passing, overhead that sounded like a large airplane but when it hit the ground, a loud noise ranged out from a long distance away. While everyone was working in their offices the sound of whatever went by left a serious noise behind. It was a loud boom and a loud rumble that ranged out all through the building. After the loud boom and rumble were over with there was a quiet feeling, which fell over the entire office building after the blast. After everything was finished outside the office building, the building is still standing but not in one piece. There are some places where the concrete from the parking lot and from other places has smashed into the building very badly. Now it's time for the real action to begin inside the building.

CHAPTER
12

ONE OF THE OFFICES on the fourth floor a beautiful woman sat at her desk as she always did every day. Her name is Ashley D. Ransnow who graduated from college six months before she started working for an architect firm in the building. Her body is so beautiful she draws attention to herself when she walks away. Her degree from college is engineering. Her body is so perfect she does not know what to do at work because every man that she has seen as hit on her for a date. Ashley noticed the only man that has not hit on her is Ted Brellon because he looks at her but no response from him. She followed Ted to his office to see where he works at in the building.

After the loud boom and rumble, she got up from her desk to look outside to see what has happened to the building after the loud noise she heard outside. Ashley draws near to the only window in the office and there was a black cloud coming towards the building. As she looks down to the ground there is a huge crater in the ground for as far she can see. She thought to herself, I wonder how far the huge crater expands. As the black cloud rolls towards the building, it made the building look like it was on fire. When Ashley finally realized what happened she told everyone in the office there is a huge crater in the ground and a black cloud, which is engulfing the whole building that she could barely see out the window. Ashley stepped away from the window people rushed to the window to see what she was talking about when Ashley looked outside. They finally decided to take turns looking outside the window for help. Ashley turned around to see someone in the corner of the same room. A woman was crying so terribly when the people in the office turned around and saw that she was about to scream. Ashley went to her to cover her mouth quickly to stop her from screaming aloud. One person was still looking outside at the time and noticed the black cloud was moving even closer to the building. She decided to tell everyone in the office so they would not get scared when they would see the black cloud in the sky again.

After Ashley had calmed down the woman in the corner she moved towards the doors to see if they could open or not. Let us speak more about the woman in the corner her name is Lisa R. Prummse and she is another beautiful woman that works in the building. She is a medium size woman that can wear anything and she would still look good. Her body is so beautiful it makes other women dull compare to her. The way she moves her body makes any man wanting her so bad that she has to turn away men. She is only looking for men that are wealthy and has a home and no wife. She wants to chase after him all she wants to because he does not have a wife at home. When Lisa finally came to her senses and realized that, she needed to be in the right mind so she can leave without getting hurt in the process. When the sprinklers went off in the office where Ashley was working at the time, she was getting wet in her nice outfit that she was wearing. When the water started, it was destroying all the files and the computers that are in the office. The water was slowly rising up from the floor after the sprinklers were on for a while.

While on another floor of the building, a man named Ted Ro. Brellon Sr., is an insurance salesman trying to make a living? Ted is a nice man who graduated from college when was 22 years old. His degree is in science but did not pursue it because he wanted to stay in his hometown and not go out of state. Ted looked around his office to see if anyone survived what had happened to the building. As he looks around the room there were a few people that did survive and they wondered what happened to the building. Ted also noticed a few people from his office did not survive. At the time, the loud boom and rumble took place some people were scared and the others were trying to find a way out of the office. After getting up off the floor in his office Ted went to the door to see if he could leave his office. The door would not move an inch and he thought to himself maybe something was jammed up against the office door. When Ted looked at the door to see if the window is big enough for someone to climb out to get help, but the only way to get out was to break the window to get on the other side of the door. Ted was looking around for something to break out the window; he noticed something odd when he was searching the room. He came across some files on one of his co-workers desks that should not be there in the first place. Ted told himself this is irrelevant to the matter at hand but I will come back to the file at a later time. He picked up a small lamp on the desk beside him. He proceeded towards the window, rose his hands up and started breaking out the window, but he could not help himself but not to think about the file again that was at his co-workers desk.

He looked out through the window and saw another door jammed up against the office door. So his suspicion was right all along about the door. Ted turned around to everybody and told him or her "they should go out the window to find a safe passageway down to the first floor and out of the building." When they left out of the office ted went back to the desk where he saw the file at so he could see why they were there in the first place. When Ted was reading over the file, he noticed some changed that he did not authorize. These people were being overcharged for their policies because somehow they were being charged $500 to $1,000 dollars more than they should be. When he finished reading the file, he decided to go ahead and leave the office so he could go find his co-worker to find out why this had happened. Ted brought the file with him so he could show his co-worker that there was something wrong with the policies that were written out for this file. Ted decided after reading the file to go ahead and climb out the window into the hallway.

Once he made it out of the office he wanted to explore the other offices on this floor to see if anyone else made it through this ordeal. Ted continued on to the next office and that door was wide open because there was nothing blocking the door. Once he entered the office, he discovered the reason why there was no debris on the outside of the office. It was because all of the debris fell on top of everyone who was in the office at the time. No one has survived in the office but what about the other offices on this floor. Ted told himself, "He couldn't take any more of seeing dead bodies everywhere." He said, "All I want is to get to the first floor and try to leave if I could in one piece." Ted could only imagine the horrible things that he would find on the other floors. Ted could not wait to make it down the stairwell to leave but first, he had to make it to the stairwell without getting hurt.

There was one person that did survive the blast in the last office that ted was in. His name is Lee Wicam Hall has been working in the office building since it first opened up in the early 1990's. He has seen people come and go in his time working here, but he has decided to do something else because he found out that his wife is cheating on him with another man in the office building where he works at. Lee does not know what he is going to do with this information right now.

Come to find out that Lee was under the desk in the far corner of the room. After Ted left the office, lee came out from under the desk to make sure that no one else is out in the hallway. When Lee noticed the man had gone around the corner he came out of the office and went the opposite way. He said to himself, "Now that I am alive and out of the office I can go down to the first floor and leave the building before anyone spots me." Lee thinks that it will be better if he waited somewhere out of the way so he can leave and go to the first floor.

Ted continued towards the other offices and found someone lying down on the floor. Ted realized that the woman that is lying on the floor was someone that worked in his office. Her name is Milly W. Zuisas who worked for him as a secretary. The only way she got the job in the office building was by her looks because she had no skill what so ever in her favor. As he knelt down to see if she was alive but sadly to say she was dead and so Ted covered her up with his coat and said a little prayer for her because he could do nothing else until help arrives. Ted continued towards the stairwell because he was afraid that everyone else could be dead.

When Ted finally reached, the door to the stairwell there was no debris in front of the door. Once Ted stepped into the stairwell, he looked up and saw huge boulders cave-in the stairs to the fourth floor. The only way for Ted to go is down the stairs to the next floor. I do not know if anyone has survived the blast on the fourth floor. He started going down the stairs to see if anyone else has survived on the other floors. Ted slowly moved down the stairs which led to the second floor but he had a hard time walking down the stairs because of all the big chunks of concrete that fell down to the floor of the stairwell. The pathway to the second floor got easier to maneuver because the chunks of concrete were getting smaller as he went down the stairs.

When Ted finally reached the second-floor door it was open a little bit, as if someone was trying to leave but couldn't because something was blocking the way. Ted looked down and saw a big chunk of concrete, which had fallen down to block the door so no one could enter or leave. He tried to pick up the chunk of concrete by himself. That is when he decided to sit down on the floor of the stairwell and use his feet to move the chunk of concrete away from the door. The piece of concrete slowly moved away from the door but it took a few minutes and also it took most of his strength out of him. Once the chunk of concrete was out of the way, Ted could now open to let someone to pass through the door so they could leave the second floor at any time. Ted decided to go check out the area on the second floor to see if anyone had made it through the blast.

CHAPTER
13

WHEN TED REACHED THE cafeteria the doors were closed normally, they stay opened until ten in the morning. Once he opened the doors, he noticed damage to the area near the doors. When he entered the room, there was something else that Ted did not expect to find. It was an enormous size boulder that went through the entire cafeteria. The whole cafeteria was completely damaged from front to back. Ted searched the area to see if anyone had survived the blast but importantly he found what seemed to be two or three dead bodies. He could not tell if it was two or three bodies because their bodies were crushed and only two faces remained intact. The two people that he did recognize worked in the building, which he has seen in the cafeteria all the time. His name is Mike Melars A. Green who worked in the mail-room while paying his way through college and he had one more year before he graduated from college. The other person was someone that he worked with in his office. Her name was Kim Mikson-Sin she has been working in the office building since the late 1990's. She has seen people come and go but she saw a young man that she would like to meet someday. Her looks are better than the average woman for her age. She has been wanting out of her marriage because there is no more romance in the marriage any more. After Ted saw all of this, he turned around and threw up what he had to eat this morning.

Ted was making his way back to the stairwell he noticed another dead body under a table next to the exit of the cafeteria. It was Rick V. Dadla from his office on the third floor. Rick was just out of high school when he started working in the same insurance office where Ted is working in the building. Rick is an average looking man for his age and build. Ted is tired of seeing all of his friends that he worked with in the build who are dead. He cannot get over what he had seen in the past few hours because most of his friends had passed away and one of his co-workers is stealing from his company. Why is this happening to me at this time?

Ted continued back towards the stairwell when he reaches the door to the stairwell. He thought to himself: I hope that I do not see any more dead bodies because I have nothing else in my stomach to throw up." Once Ted entered into the stairwell, he noticed the debris from the second floor to the first floor was minimal. When he reached the bottom of the stairwell, Ted saw the door was blown off its hinges. The door was embedded into the back wall of the stairwell.

When Ted was down by the stairwell door, he started smelling a bad odor from the lobby area. The smell was unknown to him at the moment until he walks into the lobby. Ted looked at the doorway and he noticed what seemed to be a massive area of dead people and debris all over the place. When Ted took his first step into the lobby there was a loud crunch sound down by his foot. As he looked down to the floor, he automatic stepped back because he stepped on what seemed to be a leg bone. From that, point on he watched every step that he took. Ted realized the bad smell that he smelled is that of decaying body parts and burnt human flesh. After stepping over all of the different bodies, he came across a huge fissure in the middle of the room. The biggest part of the fissure was close to the door of the stairwell, and all of the windows and glass doors were shattered into little pieces all over the ground now. Ted asked himself, "What can I do to get to the other side of this fissure so I can leave this building?"

Returning to Ashley in the office, she was trying to figure out what had happened to the building. There was something blocking the door from the outside in the hallway. Ashley screamed out they could not get out of the office, so everyone started screaming for help and no one could hear them because of the alarm that was going off in the office. As the desk went flying through the window, the glass shattered into little pieces all over the ground outside. As the desk went flying through the window, the glass shattered into little pieces all over the ground outside. The desk landed so hard it broke into small slivers of wood once it landed on the ground. The people in the office started smelling a real bad odor that would make anyone sick to their stomach. One person in the office said, "That smells like dead flesh or burnt flesh." Other people in the office said, "That is what probably happened during the blast this morning." A few people could look out the window at a time so no one would fall out of window, because they are on the fourth floor of the building. When each of them looked outside the window, they saw a large crater in the parking lot where everyone parked their cars this morning. As Ashley and the other people tried to figure out what they have to do, next so they can open the doors to their office.

Meanwhile, Ted figured out how he can get around the fissure size hole in the floor of the lobby. Ted decided that he had to find somewhere to cross the fissure without falling down the hole. It has to be the smallest gap between each side of the fissure so he could jump to the other side. It took him half an hour to find the right spot because he did not want to fall down the hole. Once Ted crossed the fissure, he found himself in front of what use to be the glass doors of the building. After looking around there was nothing else to see and do but to go outside. He noticed the ground was so fragile that when he walked on it it would crumble to pieces. As Ted walks through the area where the doors use to be he saw that the damage continued as far as he could see. Everywhere that he looked was covered in dirt, concrete, and other debris and Ted was surprised that the office building he worked in was only building standing after the blast. When he finally got outside and saw all the damage to the building, and said to himself "I am glad that some of us survived."

At the same time, Ashley figured out what to do about the jammed doors, which leads out into the hallway. She realized the hinges on the doors are on the inside of the office. Ashley looks around for something to knock out the pins from the hinges so the doors would be able to move out of the way. She found a stapler on a desk closest to her to use on the hinges. When the people in the office saw what Ashley was doing with the stapler so they took over what she was doing to the hinges. Once the pins were out of the hinges, the doors will be easier to move so everyone can leave the office. When the doors were moved away, the water that did not go out the window rushed out of the office into the hallway. When all of them stepped out into the hallway, they noticed that half the roof has caved in most of the offices on the fourth floor. None of the offices could be entered into the normal way because the cave-in of the roof. None of the offices could be entered into the normal way because the cave in of the roof. The group spread out to find anyone else alive on the floor, and to see if they can find a way out of the building. One person realized that the entrance to the stairwell was caved in; they searched for a way out to the roof. Once on the roof, they can see what is left of the area and of the building. One person from the group yelled out and said, "There is a big enough space in the ceiling where they can climb out onto the roof." But the problem was getting up to the hole in the ceiling and trying to climb out through the hole as well. They searched for a ladder but no one could find a ladder so they decided to use things to build a makeshift ladder to the ceiling. As the group searched the different offices they found chairs, desk and other things to build the makeshift ladder.

A few minutes later Ted made it outside he noticed that the people from his office were nowhere to be seen at this moment. Ted continued to make his way to the parking lot to see if the group of people made it their cars but again no one was there either. It took two hours to get to the parking lot but as Ted drawn closer to the black cloud that was radiating from the center of the crater. The smell had spread across the whole area and it stunk so bad that it made Ted vomit again and, this time, he had nothing to throw up. The black smoke was spreading so fast that Ted could not move out of the way of the cloud so he tore a sleeve off to make something that he could put around his nose and mouth. It was about two o'clock in the afternoon by his watch he walked back towards the main doors of the building. Ted noticed that someone was lying down on the ground beside the front doors. It was a person that he did not know the person that had a piece of concrete in the back of the head. That piece of concrete was so far in that only a small piece was sticking out of his head. That is when Ted bent down to search for the man's wallet so he could find out who he was. When Ted found his wallet the name on the license read Meltn Z. Hall and there is also a letter inside the same pocket and it told why Meltn was here today.

Once they built the makeshift ladder to the ceiling it took them an hour or two. When they all were on the roof, everybody looked around at the city or what is left of it after the blast. All of them were in shock seeing all of the destruction and was the surprise that the office building is still standing at all. A few people decided to sit down and try to relax a while until help arrives to rescue them. One person saw a man walking back to the front doors of the building. That same man threw a rock down from the roof to get the man's attention. At first, Ted heard something hitting the ground hard, so he waited for another rock to fall and that will tell him that someone is alive on the roof of the building. After another rock fell from the roof and he walked out far enough to look up to see not just one person but a group of people standing on the roof. Ted said to himself "Now how are they going to get down from the roof to the floor lobby?" Ted wanted to go back upstairs to see which window he can break out so he can help them down from the fourth floor to the third floor of the building.

CHAPTER
14

MEANWHILE AFTER THIRTY MINUTES of waiting for whoever was searching the offices on the third floor to leave. When Lee looked around the corner to see if anyone was in the hallway he found it was clear to precede to the stairwell. Once to the stairwell door, he peeks through the doorway to see if anyone is there to see. Lee saw that there is no one in the stairwell he proceeded to go down the stairs to the first floor of the building. When walking down the stairs he came to the second-floor door and noticed the door was wide open. Lee did not want to take any chances that someone would see him so he quietly went down the stairs. Once upon reaching the first floor it was time for him to leave the building but there was something in his way. The thing that was in his way was a huge fissure that he would have to cross over to the other side. However, wait a minute there was another way out through the back entrance of the building if it was not blocked by debris. Lee looked around to see if anyone is around, he walked towards the back of the building.

Lee thought to himself, "If my wife is alive what am I going to say to her?" Lee reached the back door, as he got closer to the door it was open enough that it could easily to be pushed open so he could leave.

When Lee stepped through the back door the sun was shining so bright, he was blinded. Once his eyes adjusted to the bright light he tried to find a way back to his house to see if his wife was alright. Lee saw that the road was no longer there but he had no choice to walk all the way home. He thought himself, "It is only fifteen blocks away I can try to walk that far to see if my house is still standing." Lee started walking down the road towards his house the first block was difficult to walk because of the terrain. The damage started to smooth out, as he got closer to his home. After resting for a few minutes Lee looked back to see how far he has walked. Lee had only walked five blocks from the office building and has not seen anyone outside walking around. He continues to the next area then he can rest again. Once it was time to rest again he realized that three hours has passed and he had only walked ten blocks. When he realized that he was only a few blocks away from his home that was when Lee decided to continue towards his home. That is when Lee decided that he could be home before nightfall. However, to his surprise, the way to his house was clear of debris. He soon realized that the street of his neighborhood was very quiet there was no one walking around or any animals are in the area. Lee figured that whatever happened has scared off all of the animals and people from the neighborhood but strangely enough, some of the neighbor's cars are in the driveway. Lee said, "Where is everybody?"

Once to his own house, Lee looked around to see if everything was alright with his home but strangely enough there was no damage to his house. Lee went to his front door to see if it was still locked and it was locked. He took his keys out of his pocket and slipped the house key into the lock. He turned the key in the lock and turned the doorknob the door opened so easily that it did not matter if anyone was home or not. Lee opened the door and stepped through the doorway to see if anything was out of the ordinary. Nothing was out of the ordinary but something was strange his wife should be home at this time of day. So far there was no sign of her yet. As Lee searched the rest of the house and noticed, he came to the master bedroom and strangely, this morning he left the bedroom door open when he left this morning. He turned the doorknob as he opens the door to the bedroom there was his wife in bed with another man. When she realized her husband made it home and he was alive she could not believe that no one heard him coming into the house. Lee asked, "What in the hell is going on?" The man was trying to leave but Lee was blocking the doorway to leave and he could not leave by the window because it was painted shut. Lee went to his office to grab his gun from his desk, and he told the man to leave while he has the chance. The man grabbed his clothes and left the house as fast as he could possibly go. When he continued towards to the bedroom, he saw the man had left already so he continued towards her, and asked how long had she been doing this? She said, "I was doing this to get your attention because our marriage is in trouble." Lee told her, "All you had to do was to come to me if you had a problem with me." She said, "I tried to talk to you but every time the subject has been changed to another topic." Well, now I am here and listening to what you have to say. She said, "I am tired of being alone at night because we don't make love any more like we use to do." Lee said, "I'm sorry about that I found out last week that you were having an affair." She said, "You have known and you did not say anything to me." I did not know what to say to you about this because I was afraid that I would do something wrong. What do you mean? I mean would I kill myself or kill you or kill both of us? Maybe we can work this out between us honey. Lee said, "I would love to try to work it out but I may be afraid that our marriage would not last long after that." She said, "What if we tried to work things out will you stay?" Yes, I would stay if we can work things out between us. So why don't we talk about things right now? Okay, sure why not. Late in the night after talking, they both decided to go to sleep for the night after eating dinner. The food in the refrigerator will probably spoil soon because the electricity is off all through the neighborhood. Maybe during the night, they can snuggle up to each other and finally be able to enjoy each other's company.

It took Ted over four hours to make it back to the third floor to see if there was a way from the fourth floor to the third floor. When Ted searched the windows on the third floor to see which windows is the best one to break so he could get a message up to them. When he picked out a window the break he searched around to see what was around the area and the only thing that he found was a fire extinguisher. As he swung the fire extinguisher, it hit the window and there was a cracking sound from the window. Ted stopped what he was doing to see what he did to the window and he said to himself, "a few more swings of the fire extinguisher to the window should break." When the window finally broke, he cleared all of the glass away from the window so he would not cut himself when he was looking out the window. Someone looked over the side of the building but still the distance from the floor to the roof was still a long way up. He signaled the person that was looking over the edge to come down to the fourth-floor window so they could talk. The person gave the thumbs up and moved away from the edge of the roof.

Twenty or thirty minutes went by and finally someone came to the window to get the attention of whoever was trying to help them. Ted heard something moving around by the window so he looked out the window to see what was going on and that is when he saw the person face less than a foot away from his face. When they both realized that, they started talking to each other so they could figure out how to get all of them down from the fourth floor. Maybe we can use the windows to help them down. Now Ted said to the other man, "Get them down from the roof and bring all of them to the window okay." The man said, "Okay." It took time for everyone to get down from the roof but just like last time it took an hour or two to get everyone down. Eventually, everyone made it to the window so the man asked everybody "is anyone afraid of heights?" Two people answered "yes, but why do you need to know?" The man said, "Because the only way down is to climb from window to window. They all agreed to go down this way because it is the only way down. Each person slowly climbed down until the very last person had to figure out what to hold on while climbing down. Ted called up to the last person to hurry up so they can all leave the building. The person bent down to tell him he has nothing to hold onto while climbing down. Ted said, "We have some strong people here that can help so put your feet over the edge so we can get a hold of your legs okay." The man said, "Okay, I will but make sure that I don't fall." "Okay," said Ted. The man slowly put his feet over the edge and two of the strongest men grabbed a hold of them and helped the man to swing his body inward towards the hallway. Finally, the man made it to the third floor in one piece so they all went to the stairwell to go down the stairs. They all made their way to the first floor but were stopped by the big fissure in the middle of the floor. Ted said, "Just follow me and I will get you across the fissure," Everyone said, "Okay, but if anyone falls we will come back to haunt you in your dreams." "Oh is that so, well I have to make sure that everyone will make it across then," said Ted.

Ted found the same spot where he jumped over the fissure before. One by one, they jumped over the fissure and made their way safely across and out the main doors. Ashley went to Ted and told him, "Thank you for getting us off the roof." Ted said, "Your welcome Ashley." You know my name I am surprised about that Ted. Oh, so you know my name as well I should think so since you do follow me to my office sometimes. Ashley could not believe that Ted noticed her following him like that to his office. Ted said, "We can talk later about what we know about each other." Ashley said, "Okay, Ted." The group finally got outside and said, "We are hungry and also need some sleep." We can move on and see if we can find food and shelter for the night but it will be fully dark about the time we do reach some place safe. Everyone said, "That is fine with us but as long as we find food and shelter for the night." It took all of them two hours to walk twelve blocks towards the center of town.

CHAPTER
15

AFTER THE IMPACT OF the large size meteor in which caused chaos for the whole area because one might not realize that a bigger disaster is headed for the area. It will take a few days before the true understanding of what happened after the meteor impacted, but at the same time, it will show that not only the impact of the meteor is only one of many things to happen soon enough. The chaos of seeing if who survived the impact and also to see if any other things will happen once the government steps in activating marshal law around the area of the impact.

With the few survivors from the building that was left alive, they came to realize that something was very wrong. Ted realized that he was being watched not up close but from afar. As he looks around to see if anything was out there but nothing was there that he could see. The fear of being watched and not knowing who is doing the watching can make anyone very nervous.

Meanwhile, Robert was still trying to figure out why everything is happening in this particular area and nowhere else in the world. Something else that was happening to Robert in which cannot be explained by any normal way other than his heritage. He knew that it was time to head towards the nearest hidden village and warn them trouble was on the way to them. Knowing this he packed up everything and checked out of the hotel and was on his way down the road to the nearest hidden village.

Robert drove for an hour and finally found the symbol that notified other members of the hidden villages that were crossing the area if they needed to stop and rest they could do that here. Robert turned down the unpaved road towards the hidden village and realized that he was being watched again. Slowly driving down the unpaved road gave a feeling of belonging but yet at the same time, it not only shows how important knowledge and understanding needs to be in this world. Robert stops abruptly because of the person standing in the middle of the unpaved road. When Robert stopped the car and got out the person in the middle of the unpaved road walked towards him and pointed towards the trees in the distance. The man never said a word but only pointed towards the trees, and Robert gathered his things from the car without saying anything either.

As Robert was walking through the trees he was met by other people from the hidden village and asked if he could speak with the elder of the village. Again no one said a single word to Robert but only pointed further inward deeper into the woods. Deep in the woods held the secrets of the past, present and future of mankind in this world. Upon entering the village he noticed symbols written on the different things throughout the village but the remarkable thing that occurred was the building in front of him. The building had his grandparent's name on it. Knowing this he went to that particular building to have a closer look at the name and it was his grandparents name alright. He raised his hand to knock on the door to see if anyone was there but before he could a man spoke to him. Please, Robert, do not knock on that door until you have spoken with the elder of our village. Robert turned around but without saying anything the man pointed towards where the elder was waiting for him.

As Robert entered the building where the elder was waiting for him several people were also sitting in the room. The strange thing was two of the people he had recognized being the hotel clerks at two different hotels on his journey from New York to New Mexico. The third person was the delivery man that had delivered the package to him one night. The other four people he did not recognize but something told him that he knew them all at one point in his life. Once Robert sat down in front of everyone the elder began by saying welcome Robert Horror. The elder points his finger to him and said, "Please be silent and do not speak until it is time to speak." As the other people in the room listens to the elder speak one thing came to his mind and it was scary in every way. That thought was he the elder has been watching him from the moment Robert left New York.

After an hour of sitting and waiting to speak he realized something was terribly wrong and it was the feeling of death is among him. Meaning it has finally dawned on him that the end is near and nobody could change the facts about what is truly about to happen in the world. The room fell silent and a single word was spoken with great understanding throughout the whole universe. That word is simple but also has the meaning in the very core of life itself and that word was DESTINY.

Robert spoke only a few words to everyone in the room and they were I am here to help. Instead of staying seated he got up and walked out of the room to go outside because he wanted to see if the building truly belonged to his grandparents or not. The symbol on the building that was his grandparents read "Family is One." But instead of knocking on the door of the building the doors opened when he spoke those words aloud. Everyone that was standing around him noticed something was different with Robert after meeting with an elder.

As the doors opened the feeling of being welcomed home from a long journey felt great but sadden because his parents are not here to enjoy this feeling. As Robert entered the building all things in him changed because now he was being welcomed with open arms by the family he never knew while growing up in the outside world. The special feeling changed from warmth of a family love to hatred in the world because as soon as he stepped into the building that held his family the large size meteor impacted Earth with the full force of multiple atomic and nuclear bombs going off. It was no longer the sadness from the villagers of the hidden villages around the area but the whole world knowing that they will not have long to live upon this world.

It has come to the attention of the elder what was happening to Robert in his grandparents building that he went to him but before the elder could enter into the building the doors closed in front of him. The elder knew what was happening inside the building but could not stop it from happening because it was too late for the world and the great warning that was needed was never heard until it was too late for all of them. Knowing this it was time to enact the final steps of ensuring the world will live on even after the escape of the alien creature from the secret bunker that was in the middle of the impact zone.

The time has come to signal all the other hidden villages that it has begun and the world needs saving once more from the doom of the vengeful alien race that seeks to destroy all other life except for theirs in the different galaxies. Meanwhile, inside the building Robert was reliving all the past family history without the full knowledge of what is happening outside in the real world. Yes, it is true that this place holds the key to survival but also it holds the key to salvation. Robert stood frozen just passed the front doorway and without fully understanding all information that has been passed down throughout the ages came to him in a moment time and it was revealed to him the true meaning of what needs to be done to save mankind and the world again. When the time is right a single word needs to be sent out throughout the world and that single word is DESTINY. The time has come to seek out the final piece of the grand puzzle which can save the world from complete annihilation. That would be the one that will lead the world into the greatest battle of all times to save mankind. When that was said the doors from the building in which Robert entered into opened and Robert stepped out and said, "It is time to send word all across the world and that word is DESTINY." Before the others could do anything the elder spoke to Robert but as he was about to speak Robert said, "I have come to help with the true knowledge of how our destiny will become once this is all over with in the near future." No other words were spoken from that moment on and the elder knew what had happened inside the building and no they have their new leader in the fight against total annihilation of mankind.

As everything was happening in the hidden village the alien creature was being released because of the large size meteor hitting the exact spot where the secret bunker was hidden from the world. The Alien creature has now been unleashed upon the world to cause havoc and also to destroy the human race. The supposed plan of the alien creature was to decrease the Earth's population enough so when the alien invasion took place it would weaken the Earth's people from responding to the alien attack. The alien's plan was to infect everyone at a certain time and date for the assurance of world domination. One way was to ensure that a sample of its blood would be studied and eventually used in every product that is needed for medical practices.

When the alien creature was unleashed upon the world it started to infect every known thing in sight because of the mission it was on. Diseases and viruses plus unknown unexplainable things have been happening once the alien creature was unleashed upon the world again. Old diseases and viruses have popped up again that were cured over the years, but this time, it wasn't just diseases and viruses that were making its way across the world.

The government was informed the moment the large size meteor impacted the area of the secret bunker. When our government was notified the moment the large size meteor hit on top of the secret bunker and it led the military to quarantine everyone in the area plus one hundred miles away from the impact site. With the knowledge from the top brass of each military branch and also the President of United States of America in a secret location that was being held in another secret bunker for protection. Yes, it is true that no matter what happens to the rest of the world some type of order and leadership must be around to ensure the safety of what is left of the world.

Now the government must stop the alien creature from becoming part of the news story that went out to the public, and the real reason behind the alien creature which is a full Alien attack. After the perimeter around the impact site and also one hundred miles around the area was completed nothing went in or came out except for military personnel. If the personnel went in they must be quarantined for a certain amount of time to see if they were infected by the alien creature. Now is the time to finally destroy the alien creature before it could cause mass harm to everyone in the world. It was too late for the government because they did not get the quarantine perimeter up in time because one person was infected but was able to leave without anyone noticing that he was infected.

CHAPTER 16

AMONG OTHER STRANGE THINGS that have happened in the area, the meteor had hit the same area as the secret bunker and the mysterious cylinder. Within the meteor impact area, the survivors were showing strange infections all over their bodies. The infections are spreading like wildfires out of control and depending on who they come into contact with it will not stop until the cause of the infections is found. With the chaos after the meteor impact is due to the crumbling debris around the site plus the survivors trying to find a way out of the area. Besides the crumbling debris, a very dark black cloud is slowly covering the whole area which will soon enough block out the entire sun in that area. This would further complicate things enough that without the sun, food, shelter or even drinkable water nobody will be able to survive the impact area.

Among the very dark black cloud comes the world worst nightmare from a long time ago and that would be the alien creature from the secret bunker and the mysterious cylinder. When the meteor impacted the secret bunker it damaged all of the controls that kept the alien creature locked up to keep the world safe from harm. Once again the alien creature has cheated death to be released upon Earth once again to cause havoc and harm to everyone in the world. Now the alien creature is free and unleashed to infect, kill or change humans into creatures that are mindless, savage and primal beings upon Earth. Within the hidden villages, the people have seen what could happen if the alien creature is released upon the world. Now is the time to send out the signal to notify all Protectors of Earth to gather for one final battle to save Earth from the alien creature.

Once the meteor impacted the government agencies responded to the area and also to quarantine at least fifty miles around the impact site. After setting up the perimeter for the quarantine area they sent in several groups to locate any survivors within the impact area. Ten full groups of five people each went into the impact area to search for survivors and one-by-one from one of the groups started to go offline and also did not respond to any calls from the command center. When that information got out to the other groups they were also being recalled back to the command center, but before they all could respond one other full group of searchers disappeared within the impact area. From a distance, the villagers from the hidden villages started to track the alien creature around the area. That is when they noticed a pattern that was left by the alien creature tracks and the tracks were straight to the command center plus into the hands of the Earth's military personnel.

The orders from command center were sent out no other military personnel was allowed into the quarantine area until every inch of it was fully searched and secured. Meaning only armed escorts could enter into the impact area and nobody else until everything was deemed searched and secured by the military. The orders came too late for the lost two groups of searchers but their lives gave the military reason to enter into the impact area with armed soldiers. Once the groups returned to the command center they were searched, quarantined and even questioned about what they saw inside the impact site. Multiple questions are to be asked and one of them did you see anything out of the ordinary while searching the main impact site? The only answer the government wanted to know was it a creature of some sorts or was it something else like a human being?

In the very center of the impact, areas held the utmost secret of all times and that would be the secret bunker which includes the alien creature. As the big dark black cloud rose high above the impact site the feeling of death, chaos, and even murder is in the air. As the wind blows the big dark black cloud in every direction it smells of dead and rotten flesh entered into a person senses throughout their body. From the meteor impact in the center, the population of the area has been reduced by fifty percent and slowly without the sun, food, water or even shelter the survivable rate will decrease every hour by two percent. The survivable rate is only a rough estimate which does not include the diseases and viruses in the same area. Since the military does not trust anyone at the impact site the survivors are left to defend themselves from harm inside the impact area.

The survivors had no way to protect themselves from harm, but out of the surrounding forest came the Protectors of Earth for the first time in history. For the first time in known history, the villagers from the surrounding hidden villages walked out among the average everyday people of Earth. Before they did so a lot more people within the area started to disappear from the surrounding groups of survivors but one thing that could not be explained which was how the people were disappearing in the first place Once they started disappearing they were no longer any traces of them afterward but also it was not just people it also included the different variety of animals. To speak more about the Protectors of Earth they fight and protect everyone from harm every from their own military force that seeks to kill anything they do not understand themselves. As the Protectors of Earth gathered all survivors that were left in the area and surrounded them for protection from the military down all the way to the alien creature that was let loose upon the world again.

As the Protectors of Earth were gathering all of the survivors the military was doing grid searches for any survivors that were still left alive in the impact area. This type of searching is slow because of how large the areas of each grid in the impact site due to the complete fifty mile s perimeter around the impact site. There a total of fifty-one grids within the quarantine impact site that will have to be searched for any and all survivors. Once the Protectors of Earth gathered all of the survivors from the area they led them all into the closest hidden village to be kept safe until everything was taken care of by them. But now the total number of survivors was less than one thousand people from the whole entire fifty-mile perimeter around the impact site. But also the other survivors could be hiding in many places trying to wait for any help from the military personnel that will ensure their own safety among them.

First, the military searched the outer twenty-five grids for any survivors before they even entered into the areas closer to the main impact site. Upon doing this every house and building that were left standing were marked with a special symbol that notifies everyone to move on because they were searched already. As the armed military and search teams moved from house to house and building to building did find a few survivors but not many at first. When nightfall came and the armed military and search teams returned to the command center with the few survivors to be tested, questioned and even held until all information were received from the survivors. The next day the search began again but they started in a different location to see if anyone else survived the impact of the meteor. They came upon what looked to be healthy survivors but one of them in the far corner looked to be very sick from something entirely unexpected and it was the chicken pox.

After finding the group of survivors they sent them to the medical testing facility at the command center to test for any abnormal diseases and viruses. The testing for any abnormal diseases and viruses which also included but not limited to other things that did not belong to the human body. After all of the testing was done they found out that none of the survivors had any mysterious abnormal diseases and viruses in their bodies. The person that looked to be only having chicken pox was in fact infected by the alien creature but like it was told before during the black plague story the alien creature made the person that was infected looked to be something else entirely. So after the testing was done all of the survivors were sent back to the main medical center to be observed over a period of time. Also, they did not realize that same person was infected and sent back to the main medical center to be observed would the other survivors to be infected also during that same trip.

With that trip to the main medical center, all of the survivors were infected and once they exited the transport vehicle they all infected other people that they encountered when they were brought into the main medical center. As the infection was spreading around the main medical center that housed sick patients were not also infected with the alien creature DNA, but also at the same time, it got back to the command center that they allowed infected people into the main medical center without fully testing them. As that was going on they started to find infected survivors closer to the center of the impact site but was unsure about how to proceed. As the orders came from the command center they are to kill and destroy all bodies in the impact area because they were infected. One Major R. L. Reyo said, "No, I will not do that some of them can be saved from the infection." The general said, "Follow your orders that you were given or you will have a court martial when you come back to the command center!" Major R. L. Reyo said, "I would rather die than kill innocent people that are not infected, but also if I am going to kill these people you better come down here and do it yourself!" Major Reyo cut off all communications between the command center and himself because he did not want to have all those deaths on his own mind.

The closer the armed military and search groups got to the inner grids the survivors are showing signs of infection from the impact site. The strange things are happening meaning people are showing all signs of the old diseases and viruses again. As the groups got closer to the main impact center site they only found maybe one percent of survivors within the center zone and also the center zone still had a big dark black cloud hanging in the air. The one percent of the survivors that were left alive in the center area of the impact site was fully infected and had no way of recovering from any infections. When the armed military and searched teams arrived at the main center of the meteor impact site they finally realized what was causing all of the infectious diseases and viruses within the quarantine area. Once they found out what was causing the different diseases and viruses in the impact area they recalled all armed military and search teams back to the command center. When everyone is accounted for from the armed escorts and search groups they now need to form a plan to contain the whole impact site from anyone going into because of the major threat that is inside of the impact site. All the other groups' responded to the command center call for retreat but again two more search groups did not respond to the call and they were also not showing any signs of life from within the main impact center site. With this information, all attack calls were given to flatten the whole area within the impact zone.

CHAPTER 17

THE METEOR UNLEASHES THE alien creature again and it also killed several people once it was released. After being released from the secret bunker every human person it encounters will either killed them or infected them with its DNA. When the alien creature infects each person that it encounters will ensure one way or another creature with its DNA will be left alive to finish the mission one way or another depending on the human military. The alien creature has to ensure that its main mission is completed before the alien invasion advances towards Earth because if the population is not less desirable the alien invasion will not work at all. When the Protectors of Earth showed up it felt the fully force presence of mankind being able to destroy it and any other less alien creature that is made from its DNA. The signal went out to every hidden village to announce the leader of the rebel army is here to defeat any and all attacks from the alien creature and the pending alien invasion that is coming soon towards Earth.

It was still hunting a way out of the area so it would not be caught or be destroyed by the military personnel within the quarantine area. As it moved through the different areas in the quarantine zone it would move in the opposite direction away from the military that wants to kill or destroy it for good because of all the harm it does to the human race. Also, the alien creature knows that the Protectors of Earth is following the alien creature to destroy it once and for all. In doing this the alien creature can lure the Protectors of Earth into the hands of the human military and then they will kill or destroy each other instead. Along the way, the alien creature moves silently along the chosen path but eventually found itself trap between the human military and the Protectors of Earth. It has come to the attention of the military and the Protectors of Earth something has to be done to protect everyone that has survived the meteor impact.

It killed multiple groups of strangely dressed humans within the meteor impact area but it was its mission to kill or change all humans into lesser beings within the world. When the alien creature sees strange looking humans in weird outfits it attacks them anyways because it wanted to ensure even though they are humans it will be a fitting process to turn them into lesser alien creatures to attack and spread the infection to the other humans in the impact area. So no one that is human will be safe from harm until all alien creatures and lesser alien creatures are terminated on Earth. Until the alien creature is killed or destroyed because there is no way to safely ensure that any human will be safe as long as the alien creature is still on Earth. In order for the alien creature to survive the impact area, it will have to figure out where to eat and find shelter to survive the harsh environment on Earth. This leads the alien creature that attacks any humans in its area, but at the same time, it is the only way to survive the harsh environment.

It is feeding off the dead human remains that are lying on the ground from the meteor impact site because it will need its strength to survive. As the alien creature roams the impact zone looking for survivors it feeds off of dead bodies lying on the ground. In doing this it was ensured that its survivable rate will increase because that it is feeding and not starving for food while it was hunting the humans within the impact zone. Every time the alien creature turned a human into a lesser alien being it gave orders to head towards the command center and attacks anyone that it encounters. In doing this it will confuse the military army that they had killed the real alien creature but instead, it will be killing all the lesser alien creatures that were once a human. While the human military army is busy with all the lesser alien creatures their attention will be diverted to protect their own command center from harm.

It is killing again away from the center impact zone and this time, it also infected a group of survivors in that area. As the alien creature was moving inside the impact zone it decided to infect everyone that it encountered but also it realized that no matter where it went the Protectors of Earth and the human military will track it down. As the Protectors of Earth are closing upon the alien creature sensing that the end is near for some of them they still risked their own lives to save others in the world. Robert finally realized the only way this alien creature can be dealt with is for all the survivors to move out of the impact area completely. Once all of the survivors are completely gone then it will head towards the nearest place where some more humans are gathering away from the impact area. The cycle of killing, feeding, and even changing the humans to lesser alien creatures will continue until every last human is changed.

The alien creature was trying to get as far away from the secret bunker that was hidden underground holding the alien creature for so long because it would do more harm to the human than anything else in the world. The fear of returning back to the secret bunker drove the alien creature to leave the impact zone for its own survival because it needed to ensure that no matter what happens it can continue on its mission. As the alien creature continues to run away from the secret bunker not realizing that the secret bunker is no longer usable because of the meteor hitting the same area. No matter what happens the alien creature must finish its mission because the alien invasion force depends on the outcome of the attack so they can strip the Earth of all the resources to further invade any other habitual worlds. The time has come to understand every last detail about the truth behind why the alien creature is truly here on Earth and not somewhere else in the vast galaxy. The further understand why the alien creature needs to leave the impact area completely before it dies trying to accomplish its mission.

The further away the alien creature got from the impact zone and the secret bunker it got scared as to the humans will accomplish their goals to kill him with everything they got in their own arsenal. The alien creature held the key to infecting more people when it was trying to seek shelter from the military that wanted to kill it but instead of killing the humans it only infected them instead. The only understanding that it had was to cause a mass panic from killing, infecting and even changing the human DNA to alien DNA for better control of Earth. As it was trying to locate better shelter to stay safe from the human military before the full attack force of the alien invasion that is coming towards Earth at a fast pace. As the alien creature moves about within the impact zone it sensed trouble times for the survivable rate for itself and the others like it but in truth, it is a low survivable rate because it needs lesser alien creatures to occupy the human military force. The alien creature still searched for other humans to transform into lesser alien creatures to help out in infecting other humans on Earth.

Again the alien creature saw more people dressed in strange outfits that were searching all of the different buildings in the area. The military sent in more searchers to search for survivors but did not learn from the first two groups that were killed by the alien creature. The military is always trying to show how forceful they are but in truth, they are only trying to conceal everything from the public because they do not want a mass panic spreading throughout the world. The alien creature is getting closer to the outer perimeter of the quarantine zone but also at the same time, it feels the need to kill every last military soldier in its path. In doing this it will ensure the path of destruction it leaves behind will scare any other personnel under the military command. The alien creature moves closer and closer to the outer perimeter zone to finally see how many people are truly in the area for many reasons beyond any human understanding of the problem.

Finally getting close to the outside perimeter of the quarantine area, and it is waiting for nightfall before trying to cross the perimeter field to leave the impact area. As the alien creature was getting closer and closer to the outer perimeter of the impact area it was trying to study the different patterns from the humans. If the truth be told the alien creature has to understand why that the feeling of killing, infecting and even changing the DNA of all humans is necessary to collect all the resources from Earth. As the alien creature searches for any weakness towards the perimeter so it can enter without being seen and then slip through undetected plus start infecting all the military soldiers in the area. In the understanding of how the alien creature thinks and acts towards all of the mankind is because it was breed into it for many reasons. With the understanding of how intelligent the alien creature truly is just one factor of the problem because of the way, it wants to get pass the outer perimeter zone.

When crossing the perimeter field it infected two guards and turned them into a lesser alien creature form. The alien creature uses the two turned guards to cause a distraction among the military personnel. Instructing the two known lesser alien creatures to turn on their own military friends to kill them, eat them, infect others and even turn them into lesser alien creatures. While it changed the two humans and gave them instruction to cause a distraction among the military and also the alien creature slowly entered the command camp to see what was there to begin with in the first place. It slowly slipped passed the outside perimeter and into the military camp and it realized something was wrong and went back into the quarantine area again. It sensed something was wrong when all of a sudden they turned on him and opened fire with everything they had in their arsenal.

Even though it was hit multiple times on its body it grew in size and strength but at the end, it turned around and left the command camp due to the understanding of how the human military force works now. The reason behind it leaving the military command camp was because it sensed a Protector of Earth that had more power than normal. The alien creature finally knows fear for the first time in history but now it must continue to amass a huge army by changing the humans into lesser alien creatures. Running scared from the Protector of Earth it realized that the people from all that time ago were still around waiting for the chance to finish off the alien creature. This time, it kills, infects and even turns some more humans into alien creatures to cause more chaos around the impact site. This time, it will not stop until every human within the impact area is changed to a lesser alien creature to increase its odds in winning the war against mankind.

CHAPTER
18

AS THE PEOPLE FROM the damaged office building are trying to recover from what happened with the meteor hitting the area they were just trying to survive the night without dying. Knowing full well that at any moment in time either one of them can die from starvation, killed from falling debris or even worse the military can come in and send them to the command center for testing. In doing the last one the group would never be able to finally reach home. As the group sits around in a group they realize that the only way out of the problem is to sacrifice a few for the greater good of the group. Some share this idea but others do not because of what is being aid over the loud speaker every thirty minutes. Since the survivors realize the military has quarantine anyone inside the quarantine area they will not be able to leave without some type of help from either inside the quarantine area or even from outside other than the military.

Besides the main group one or two people have mysteriously vanished from the group and the area itself. As the first night went on the group started to realize that more and more people are vanishing from the group and the close net friends are starting to worry about if it is the military or something else that is causing the problems. The message over the loud speaker had change and now it was saying please out into the open area for us to come and retrieve you for transportation to the command center for evaluation. No harm will come to those are survivors from within the quarantine area. Everyone in group feared that if they were to do what the military wanted them do they would all die one way or another depending on the outcome of evaluation.

The group took a vote and all but two refused to even think about what the military will do to them once they appeared out in the open. The others will remain in hiding until they can be rescued by other means necessary. When the truth is told the survivor now only have thing in common and that is to survive at all cost. Since it is getting darker by the hour no one can now wonder around to find the necessary things for survival because it is too dangerous for people at this moment. The group has chosen a leader and his name is Ted but right now at hand is to ensure everyone has enough water, food and warmth during the night. Without the proper survival gear no one will be able to survive in the harsh conditions within the quarantine area.

When and if the group can survive the night it will be up to them to find shelter, power, water, food and even survival gear for all of them to survive more nights until help can come to save them all. Each person of the group encounters surplus stores in the area can finally gather everything they need to survive the area until help arrives. It took three surplus stores until everyone finally gathered all the supplies that were needed but at the last surplus store they noticed a lock back room. Once the lock back room was opened there was enough weapons, ammunition, combat gear for a full invasion force against anything from law enforcement and military agencies. The surviving group is now down to fifteen people after the fourth night of surviving the quarantine area.

Instead of other people joining the main survival group the want to prove they can provide protection for themselves and the other in their own group from harm. There were gun fights and people killing other people for their survival gear equipment but in doing so it reduces their own chances for survival in the quarantine area. As the mysterious creature watches will waiting for the different chances in changing the human into lesser alien creatures all it had do too was to wait long enough all the humans will kill each other without his help in conquering the world. By reducing the world population greatly even before the main invasion force can reach Earth the alien creature will have no problems in completing their main goal in retrieving resources to further other worldly attacks in the galaxies.

As the alien creature is watching the human kill themselves it also has to try and warn the pending alien invasion force that it was still trying to complete its own mission. The Earth modern day electronics are still not advanced enough for it to send any signal beyond the Earth's atmosphere. Without having all the parts that is needed it still had to wait until the alien invasion force is closer to Earth. The only goal for the alien creature is to extract lesser alien creatures for a small army and to cause mass panic on the world. Once the human population is small enough the alien invasion force can wipe out all leftover human for the control of the planet. Every night some more people have been vanishing from the group again but this time they circled back to and find them again but in doing so they found one person from there group. That one person from the group is dead from what seems to be an animal bite to the throat. None of the survivor gear was even touched or used during the night and what is strange in the matter his weapon was never fired or drawn from the gun holster.

Two different answers can come from this the first is he knew his attacker or the second is the attacker surprised the survivor and then killed him instantly. The understandings of both scenarios are possible but at the same time, it could not be understood as to why someone or something would kill him and leave all his gear intact. Only one plausible explanation is they are being hunted down and killed for only one reason and that reason is simple leave no survivors behind. Meaning leaving survivor behind will eventually give others the whereabouts of the hunter in the area. As if the vanishings are not enough to worry about now they have to watch where they are going because of the major threat to their own survival.

The reactions from the military towards the mysterious vanishings are simple stop all searches within the quarantine area for further survivors. The reason behind this is to protect everyone that enters into the quarantine area from harm before finding the true cause behind the vanishings. When the military realized that the vanishings were happening in the quarantine area only they finally realized something was happening inside that is causing the vanishing and now everything is going very wrong for everyone. Slowly the majority of the survivors that were left in the quarantine area are in fear for their own safety. As the military reduces the quarantine area from fifty mile radius to thirty mile radius will give them an advantage to finding more survivors and also the cause behind the mysterious vanishings.

The command center finally has some of the test results from the first few survivors and none of them are showing any signs of infection from inside the quarantine area. But from the second group of survivor's closer the meteor impact site are showing signs of infection. The first group of survivors will be transported to a full medical hospital for a more detailed analysis of their body. When the first group of survivors left the command center one out of eight survivors became very ill within only one mile of the medial hospital. Before the survivor could be restrained it had bitten the other survivors and the transport guards. As the attack was happening the infected survivor jumped out of the moving transport vehicle and escaped towards the closest town from the medical hospital.

When the command center was notified by the other escort vehicle the general realize that all survivors must be killed and burned. Now they have one escape infected person and a whole lot of survivors inside the quarantine area that could also be infected by whatever it is inside the quarantine area. The black cloud that is still hanging above the quarantine area is now being tested for the reason behind the infection, but no one realized that the dark black cloud is not the source of the infection. The dark black cloud was only the cover for the alien creature to escape its own prison from within the secret bunker that was hidden underground long time ago. The belief of the government and the survivors the military will only be responsible and the understanding anyone that is infected must be killed and burned in order for the protection of the world.

The announcement went over the loud speaker that any survivor approaches any military personnel they will be shot on sight because they all are infected from an unknown source inside the quarantine area. From that moment on all survivors must band together in order to escape and survive the onslaught of mass murder from their own government and military personnel. Now is the time for leadership to survive an annihilation from the military and whatever I killing them inside the quarantine area. The spilling of blood by the government is just another way for them to ensure no survivors and no explanations can be sent out into the world. To the government and the military it is just another training exercise in case a meteor truly did hit Earth in the near future. But unbeknownst to the world the infected survivor has now achieved its goal to infect as many more people once out into the open areas of the world.

As the military is killing survivors from the command center and inside the quarantine area now people are being killed by their own government and also the alien creature inside the quarantine area. Besides the alien creature killing humans it is also turning some to lesser human in which they can be controlled by higher alien creatures upon the time the alien invasion force has started to attack Earth. Since the military had reduced the quarantine area to thirty mile radius around the impact site more strange sighting has been occurring close to the perimeter edges. The understanding about the survivors something has to be done to protect everyone else outside the quarantine area because it will simply not be enough to ensure our own government that no harm will come to the rest of the world from anything inside the quarantine area.

CHAPTER 19

EVEN WITH THE MILITARY killing the survivors inside the quarantine area the lesser alien creatures are killing them also not just for sport but for a food resource to survive the new world. In the understanding on how the military reacts towards all known hostiles they shot first then ask questions later but for now it's just trying to kill them all for the survival of mankind. It is up to the survivors within the quarantine area to ensure their own safety until they can figure a way out of the quarantine area without being killed. What was later witnessed by two survivors was how the lesser alien creatures can now transform back into a healthy looking human at will but now it was not just a human being it also looked like a military man. The two survivors witnessed something that has never been seen before but now feared that Earth will not be able to survive whatever is happening on Earth anytime soon.

The two survivors kept watching the military man walking closer to the perimeter that surrounded the quarantine area but eventually it walked up to the perimeter gate and was allowed inside the command center. The two survivors noticed that the alien creature walked among the other military soldiers inside the command center without even being stopped to see where he came from inside the quarantine area. After the alien creature was inside the command center for an hour things started to happen to all of the military soldiers. Now you have to realize that this command center was one of five that surrounds the whole perimeter but also if one side of the perimeter is destroyed any lesser alien creatures can simply walk pass them all and continue on towards the rest of the world without being stopped by anyone. After three hours have passed the whole command center was now under the lesser alien creature control. The others were signaled to come towards the command center that was attacked and it was time to conquer the rest of Earth before the alien invasion force arrived.

In doing this only one lesser alien creature stayed behind to ensure any other human being that was left alive would die so the other lesser alien creatures can ensure world annihilation. If and when the quarantine area gets smaller in any way the military force will realize that one of the command centers was destroyed from inside the command center gates. The survivors will be in danger from the military because they will be blamed for the killing of the military soldiers and all of the survivors left inside the quarantine area would be killed. With of the new lesser alien creatures that are now roaming the command center it was time to exit and go out into the world to finish their mission of world annihilation. As the lesser alien creatures spread across the United States old diseases and viruses are popping up everywhere but what is really worse the lesser alien creatures are expanding rapidly.

With the growth of the lesser alien creatures expanding more and more animals plus other human being are starting to vanish from sight. As the days turns into weeks the count of alien creatures around the United States has grown too fast for any of the military to react towards them. In truth the final days seems to be coming not from space but from the Earth itself. With no way to counteract the alien creatures now trying to dominate Earth because of the vital resources it has to offer them. It seems that Earth has no way to protect itself from harm even with the advancement in military technology. More alien creatures are appearing all over the world now and slowly the world population has decreased by twenty-five percent over a two month period of time. The reduction was of course caused by the old diseases and viruses plus the alien creature turning humans into lesser alien creatures. The order has finally comes down the line that every human left to fight must fight to save mankind from annihilation.

With the understanding that anyone with the will to fight for our freedom must fight and kill every last one of the alien creatures even though they use to be our own friends and family. It is time that we as humans takes back our Earth and ensure we survive at any cost possible. The possibility in surviving the battle to save Earth will come at a high price but to ensure mankind survives this fight it was time to bring out the new weapons, armor and even military vehicles. In doing this it will show the alien creatures we will not go down without a fight to save all of humanity. The very possibility of losing everything that mankind has done over the centuries must finally come to the point of how much should one person give before everyone has to ensure the safety of mankind that will hopefully last for eons.

The destiny of mankind is always in turmoil because of the different choices they make in each of their own lives. The understanding that one choice can alter the lives of others can ultimately unbalance the whole entire world because of one choice was made for greed and profit instead of protection for every human being on Earth. In truth with the way mankind has been going greed and profit will indeed guide the way towards the full destruction of Earth. The knowledge and understanding of how some people on Earth is guided towards money, power and even status given the right opportunity to gain such items in life.

With the understanding of how mankind is viewed from all over the world is that our society is money and power driven in all aspects from the moment each person comes into contact with money. The truth is something that some people do not want to believe but with this understanding all of our lives are intertwined until the time will come that money no longer drives our souls. Eventually the time will come that we must learn how to protect ourselves from harm in every possible way. Upon the strange feeling of being watched from the sky now has come true because of the strange things happening in our sky.

The attention towards the sky has become more intense because of the weird signals coming towards Earth. In this it only means that eventually more alien creatures are coming to ensure the human race is fully annihilated to achieve their own goals of stripping every last usable resource from this planet before moving on. It seems now is the time to either quietly hide or fight for the survival of mankind.

CHAPTER 20

THE DIFFERENT GOVERNMENTAL RUN signal stations around the world are picking up some strange non-verbal type communications. Inside the unknown strange non-verbal type communications are unexplained command codes in which are being transmitted to some unknown person or place on Earth. It is time to locate where the signals is heading towards on Earth because somewhere on Earth has to be the reason behind the strange unknown communications. Locating the receiver will help the military to destroy the receiving location and all receivable information to stop what is happening. Sometime things are stranger than facts and the strange facts in this case the communications are in one language only and no others. There are no known languages added to the strange unknown language being transmitted towards Earth. While communicating the different codes in the one language is strange because normally communications are transmitted in multiple languages across the board. For the mysterious codes no one in the military themselves has yet to decipher or break the coded mysterious messages that are being broadcast. In truth they have never heard of this type of language before now because most of the codes that has been recorded over time had been recorded for communication purposes for the military, and the reason behind this is simple everyone has certain types of codes they use from their own country to hide things from everyone one else.

Since the codes are repeating themselves over and over it seems that one of them must be a command code because it is seeking the correct response code that goes along with the different messages. Without the proper response it will alert the alien invasion force that the alien creature has failed in its mission. The signal station finds out the strange command codes is coming from on the other side of moon but in truth the signal is coming from somewhere past Saturn. As the signal is getting stronger means whatever it is the signal is getting closer to Earth. Since the direction of the signal is coming from is pass the far side of the moon it shows the intercept course of the mysterious objects. In the government logic which they did not believe what the scientists were saying they had to their own assessment of the problem. The government finally they had to trace the signal to see where it was coming from and the actual direction of the signal. When the direction of the signal was located they realized the intercept course was getting closer to Earth. Strange enough the signal has one other thing embedded in the coded messages and that is also a countdown code with it besides the command codes. The countdown code has a certain amount of time added to it and it reads forty-eight hours until whatever is supposed to happen after the time runs out. Strange enough once the countdown clock started somehow it activated a nuclear warhead from one of the underground facility. Without knowing the truth behind the origin of the different codes it is a real threat of global annihilation. All governmental signal stations are trying to decode all of the messages as fast as they can which in turn can hinder their own response towards the pending doom of Earth.

When the messages started coming over the intercom system one lonely person that is a Protector of Earth realized that she recognized the language which she was able to decode all of the messages. As she was listening to the coded messages it was her chance to inform her people that the ending doom heading towards was in fact the same type of alien creature they have been hidden all of the centuries ago. While decoding the messages it will give her people a greater edge for the coming Alien Invasion force to stop them before any more harm can be done to Earth's population. As she decodes the messages and recoded them into her own language for the elders of each hidden village can relay to their people to prepare for war that is heading towards them right now. The coded messages has a date and time of when the attack is to take place against Earth's planet which also includes how they are attack Earth. Once the messages were ciphered back into her own language it was time to leave without being notice by anyone inside the building as she was leaving the text was sent to the person waiting for her outside to pick her up and leave the area fast without anyone noticing.

After leaving with her the driver made one phone call to someone close by the main hidden village that the gathered all of the high elders from all five hidden villages around the area. It took four hours before she had arrived to the main hidden village that housed all of the high elders from the five different hidden villages. Once she arrived the lady was escorted to where the high elders were waiting for her to arrive with the messages. After the high elders received the coded messages and they realized that the time has come to prepare for the worst. Her elder was waiting for the coded messages to be deciphered again and relayed to all Protectors of Earth. When the elder receives the coded messages the next logical step is to inform everyone within the five hidden villages around the area. After decoding all of the messages the truth about the pending alien invasion was true.

Once the messages were deciphered again the elder realized how dangerous things will be for everyone on Earth. Now is the time to seek a new leader for all of the Protectors of Earth and people hidden within the five different hidden villages around the area. When the high elders realized the only person capable of leading them towards victory and that person would be Robert Maxwell. Meaning it was time to inform Robert about the different deciphered messages with the different messages decoded Robert realized it was time to draw up battle plans for everyone. The battle plans must include every way to protect everyone around the world but also include the safety of the villagers. For the villagers that wish to fight alongside of the Protectors of Earth must learn how to fight accurately and professionally as well. The battle plans also includes formation, attach strategies and what types of weapons being used in the battle. Protectors of Earth are getting ready for a battle between humans and the alien invasion force heading towards them. Protectors of Earth must be fully battle ready for the alien invasion force. In preparing for a war they all must realize it may be a one way ticket to their graves. Time to learn all the new weapons and tactics for fighting the alien invasion force to save mankind from annihilation.

The time has come to gather all of the necessary equipment and survival gear for all fighters and Protectors of Earth to protect everyone from harm. It is time to retrieve everything needed for training because of the pending battle and by bringing all of the necessary equipment and other gear to one location to ensure the proper planning is achieved for the battle against the alien invasion force. One central location will be used to house, train and produce everything that is need to ensure some type of survival after the alien invasion force. There will be daily training for everyone in the centralized hidden base because it will give everyone one of them protection from harm if they get injured during battle. Multiple training sessions with everyone that is involved with the battle from the beginning to the end. The daily training comes with a high price because the strongest will last longer than the others that are training on a daily basis.

The necessary protection for everyone in the five different hidden villages but that too will not be able to happen in real life either. For many reasons known among the elders in each of the hidden villages can only be provided if they have some Protectors of Earth stay behind to protect the young and weak. The main reason is the hidden villages are too wide spread around the area of the secret bunker. It is time to withdrawal into the hidden fortress deep in the forest that is three miles to the west of the secret bunker. Now is the time to move everyone and everything to the fortress because it may be the only way to protect everyone from being killed including all of the humans. To fully understand the fortress is to fully understand the complexity of how and why the fortress was built in the first place. In the long run hiding within the fortress can help for short term only because of how they must fight the alien invasion force heading towards Earth. It will give about a quarter of the Protectors of Earth the chance to stand guard over the rest of the villagers. The rest of the villagers need a chance to find out what role they will play in the battle to save Earth from total annihilation. In speaking the truth only one survivor needs to be left alive to tell this story and that would be the youngest of the Protectors of Earth and the youngest Protector of Earth is called Sarah Josephine Cater.

CHAPTER
21

THE SIGNALS ARE INCREASING by two every hour and the decoders are sending the governmental scientists signs we are not alone. The signals are showing the different governmental scientists they are now not alone in the universe. The fear that we are not alone is growing greatly because of the unknown objects heading towards them. Even though the decoders are trying their best to decode most of the messages but yet they are still unable to decipher any of the messages at this time. The decoders are using every ciphers they ever had used from the beginning of time when any person was using ciphers around the world. But in truth with all of the different types of deciphers around the world none of them are working to crack the coded messages that are coming across the intercom. The messages are in a complex language that no one seems to understand besides the Protectors of Earth.

Now the scientists finally believes that we are not alone in the universe and it goes to show that no matter what we think about the universe it will always prove to us that we are wrong. With all of the information pouring into the signal station from the different satellites in Earth's orbit none of it reveals the true origins of the coded messages. The scientists and other governmental agencies not knowing the language or true origins of the messages that is being transmitted no one will be able to decipher any of the messages in time to stop anything from happening towards Earth. The harder they try to decode any of the mysterious messages the more confusing they become for the decoders. In every possible way to decode any of the messages by using the different codes that were made over the centuries from the beginning when words were formed showed no actual answers to any of the mysterious messages. By using the old codes to decode the mysterious codes shows complete non-sense by anyone using these mysterious coded messages. Another strange thing that had happened no one realized that someone as left the room without being seen. How can this person leave a locked room without being allowed out of the room by security themselves? The room is in total lock down because of the mysterious coded messages could mean that Earth is in total danger by an unknown source other than themselves.

As the code breakers work to figure out the mysterious coded messages by trying different techniques to decode all of the messages they finally realized they had failed completely. The confusion continues because nobody knew how to decode the messages. From that moment on they must prepare their military for any possible attack from any unknown source that is heading towards Earth. The truth of everything happening in this room must remain confidential and quiet until the source can be confirmed by satellites and other means around the world own by the military. While using many different deciphering techniques that has been used since the beginning of forming words in the world they noticed one key factor with the problem at hand. The problem at hand is that the coded messages are not of this world but other worldly position because of how no one can decipher any of the mysterious coded messages.

Since this has now become an act of war it is time to arm every military compound around the world for an attack of an unknown origin heading towards Earth. Every military base is called to active duty to protect the citizens and the world from harm. When the orders from Washington D.C. came into play they realized something was totally wrong and what would make them decide to prepare for war when no other country is doing the same. That question and many others will have to wait and see what truly happens when the signal is made to move towards the approaching army that is trying to annihilate everyone on Earth. Being prepared for something that may never come but yet being ready for battle must be understood in every way around the world.

Finally the scientists triangulated where the signals are coming from and they are coming from the far side of the moon. The signals is moving straight towards Earth at a slow rate of speed and besides noticing that they also noticed the signals are getting closer and closer towards Earth. Somehow the rate of speed for the signals is getting faster than before the military first heard them six months ago. As they try to figure out the configuration the rate of messages being received on Earth versus the rate of speed for the messages being sent towards Earth. Since whatever is sending the mysterious coded messages has now tripled in speed because the objects are getting closer to Earth's orbit. No matter what the problem is the only way out of it is to fight to the death because of how things are turning out to be with mankind all over the world. To fully understand the complete reasons behind the signals coming from the mysterious objects can only prove to be one thing. We are not alone in this universe or others across the vast expanse and also in the total vast entirely multiple universes.

In calculating the distance between the mysterious messages being sent from the far side of the moon to Earth and the scientists found that the distance was only three days away. Slowly with every calculation being done to ensure they have enough time to prepare for battle it is not too late because in seventy-two hours from this moment on whatever is approaching Earth will be here soon. Every moment they waste in preparing for battle gives the mysterious objects time to maneuver into position around Earth. As the distance is closing slowly but fast enough to alarm every military base around the world. The alarm has been sounded around the world to prepare for the danger that is approaching Earth. In doing this it has caused a mass panic among the public around the world. In truth the mass panic has been happening ever since there has been communications among the CB and ham operators/handlers. Meaning, little bits of information has been going out around the world to inform them about what is happening at the different military bases. It is all leading up towards an invasion from another country or even something bigger is happening in our world. No one is sure of what is truly heading towards us because of all the lies that our own government has been feeding us over the years.

It has come to the attention of the Protectors of Earth that in twenty-four hours from now all of the nuclear missiles around the world will be fired towards any high volume area full of people. Knowing this will increasingly give the ultimate surprise for everyone around the world because of one simple fact. That simple fact is not just the alien creature that was being held in the secret bunker but a total new threat has been found out the hard way. Someone or a group of people as been in place to activate the nuclear warheads from the different consoles around the world plus in realizing this now it is too late to stop the nuclear warheads and the alien invasion force from attacking Earth. Another way for the nuclear warheads to be activated is by the command countdown code that was embedded inside the mysterious messages and the governmental signal station entered the mysterious messages into their own computers in turn activated the launch codes for the nuclear warheads. No matter if they had the proper deciphering codes to stop this from happening it was already too late because once the messages were entered into the computer system it activated the sequence of events from the beginning. With this growing threat unrealized within the governmental signal station with every new data that comes from the orbiting satellites can now show an increasing amount of mysterious objects heading towards Earth not just a single object.

With high orbit satellites pointing towards outer space the truth has come to light and now pointing them towards the moon inside the images which is showing multiple mysterious objects heading towards Earth. There are hundreds of the mysterious objects heading towards Earth from what the images are showing everyone searching for the truth behind the mysterious objects and messages. Besides believing the lies now comes the truth for everyone to see in full view in the very blue sky. Now is the time to pray towards the heavens for protection in every possible way for safety of the pending doom heading towards Earth.

CHAPTER 22

SINCE THE SATELLITES ARE sending information back towards Earth showing what the mysterious objects might be but without fully knowing what is going on the United States military is on full active alert. The problem with satellite images coming back towards Earth it will take time to fully explore what the images could be but also at the same time, it will lead the government in trying to protect everyone from harm. As the scientists from the U. S. Government tries to understand the images and information it is leading them down a path of regrets for everyone in the world. To fully understand everything that is truly happening to them around the world they must first realize that everything that has been kept hidden from the rest of the world for so long has now began to unravel. In truth the only way for the world to might recover from the pending doom that is heading towards them is to embrace that a full out assault on whatever is approaching in hopes to protect them from being killed or wiped out of all existence.

With all the information and images that is being relayed to the different U. S. Governmental agencies to confirm all incoming data in which is finally showing that we are not alone in the universe anymore. After days of studying the different images and information a single object is moving faster than the others. The object that is moving faster than all others have something strange about it meaning it is leaving a trail behind itself so the other mysterious objects can follow its path towards the surface of Earth. As the minutes turns into hours then the hours turn into days the feeling of not being alone anymore has grown to a great fear for their own survival. Soon within a couple of days the largest mysterious object will be in viewable range enough to see what is truly heading towards Earth at a fast rate of speed. In another few hours the full view of the mysterious object will be insight for everyone to see.

Now as for the government thought was the best secret of the whole world was now out for the people on Earth to truly know that we are not alone in the universe. The secret of space flight with mysterious object for the basis of learning from that has been covered up since the early 1950's that our own government wants nobody to know. In knowing this the government only has one option left to enact for ensuring the world to be free for then to now the biggest secret of them all. Since the secret is finally out each government around the world will inform their own people that some mysterious objects are heading towards Earth. Once the information was finally sent out to the majority of the world it was now up to the government to find a way to communicate to the approaching mysterious object. In truth the mysterious objects heading towards Earth has no reason to communicate their true intentions to Earth because to the alien creatures no human life is worth saving.

Around the world mass panic ensue everyone to find shelter from harm but it would be too late because the governments around the world have dragged their feet that can ensure safety for everyone around the world. When the mass panic started it sent everyone around the world in a spin because now no one is safe from harm. Death, murder, crime of passion are among the biggest part of the mass panic to purge the people that has caused grief and trouble even before the mysterious objects approached Earth. The world was plunged into chaos because of the mysterious objects that are heading towards Earth, but to see the full extent of the cause it was the people of Earth blaming the only known people they could and that would be their own government.

The human race has for centuries blamed other people for their own problems in the world but to finally get the feeling the people of Earth has finally come to believe they were right all along. Some people are calling this the end of days that was stated in the Bible. Now churches, communities and even people that believe in GOD the almighty has to come to the finally realization that only the righteous people of GOD will survive the end of days. In the coming days of the pending doom for everyone in the world they will try and kill each other to prove their worth to either Satan or God. The reason for this is they themselves want to live a full life before it is time to meet each of their makers. In understanding if the bible is correct there will be wars, famine, death and even a new supreme leader. In the bible it does say that each of these will be shown as the four horsemen of the apocalypse. Now the book of Revelations has different meanings and understanding as to the final days of Earth but in truth one of many understandings behind this can also lead each of us down another path entirely.

The first is the multiple wars around the world that will bring chaos and also other strange things that are only known to a select few around the world. In the bible wars could mean anything from wars to gain other territories more food, more medicine and maybe even more control over military forces. Yes, it is true that war will influence the different parts of the world but also it will change how things are done within the world itself. Now after wars have started or even ended in many areas around the world it can leave the other places in a famine without resources to sustain life as we all know it. Without resources the weakest people will die and the strongest will survive because the strongest people now control the flow of resources to vital parts of the world. Now this can have other problems to show up a new leadership put into place to stop all wars and battles around the world. Now the time has come to start with one nation and even one type of currency around the world. In truth the wars, famine and a new leadership on Earth will also lead towards a single ruling government over everyone around the world. With new leadership comes with a price that has to be paid in full because in order for Earth to come out of chaos an understanding that must be known to everyone that wants to life in the new world. New laws, new rules, and even new leadership has a price to be paid for living in the world that is willing to give food, shelter, water and other resources to those who will obey the new world order. The punishment for even disobeying the new world order is death, and with that understanding a new society will be formed to control the vast amount of people still left alive on Earth.

Before anything about the new world order to be activated they must survive the pending doom heading towards that is about to approach Earth's atmosphere. The fear that everyone is facing is the fear that their own time has come to an end for them and for everyone else on Earth. The only hope that Earth has been the people slowly steering them into the actual understanding how they can survive the alien invasion force heading towards them as they speak. Now is the time for each one to understand the importance of survival in today's society from anything that can be harmful. People all over the world are now saying that Earth is doomed and nobody is safe anymore, but finally some of them are no longer worrying about their own life. Now they are worrying about the lives of the children and all others that cannot defend themselves from harm.

CHAPTER
23

THE FEARS ARE GROWING rapidly because of the mysterious objects heading towards Earth. In the eyes around the world, it shows how none of us is ready to die. So now the fears of the people are becoming true in the very sense of the word. In truth, the time has come for everyone to pray toward God and the heavens for forgiveness. Now is the time for the Protectors of Earth to emerge from hiding to protect everyone. The Protectors of Earth and all of the other fighters are asking to join in the war to save all of mankind. The chaotic atmosphere has started to boil over into the real life world. The world is growing ever so rapidly into a chaotic place that no one is safe from harm. There are mass killings around the world to safeguard their freedom into hell by satisfying the need to the devil. So now it would seem the final days or what the Bible calls Armageddon. Even though the mysterious objects are moving closer the world is not paying attention to the major threat that is already in the world. The major threat is the actual alien creature that is still inside the quarantine area. Of course, the quarantine area is only for the safety of the survivors that will ensure they are free of contamination.

The alien creature is still within the quarantine and also doing harm to everyone it sees. Since the alien creature is still in the quarantine area causing havoc and is still infecting plus killing humans to become lesser alien creatures. In truth, the alien creature is still trying to accomplish its mission on Earth. Without fully knowing the extent of what really would happen because of the government allowing the alien creature to accomplish its mission without being stopped. In doing so soon enough all of the lesser alien creatures are let loose upon the military holding the quarantine area in place. The threat has become real with no way out but fighting to save mankind or die trying, either way, it will be hard. The only way to safeguard mankind is to train everyone with the full ability to fight. This means we can no longer be able to say no one under the age of eighteen or even over the age of sixty can no longer stay out of the fight. The time has now come for the truth behind the alien creature and also the alien invasion force heading towards Earth. Finally, the truth is somewhat told to the public about what is happening to our world. Each government around the world is only telling half of the truth and the other half are complete lies at face value.

The true origins of the alien creature and the invasion force have found by the direction of the mysterious alien spaceships. Strange enough from the direction of the alien spaceships is showing the origin of the alien creature home planet in an actual solar system that was already charted by an unmanned satellite probe which sent back information in real time. The computer information is showing that only non-manned probes can survive the journey because in earth years it would take one thousand years to reach the system. The unmanned probe was finally lost as it struck a planet with some type of electronic signals coming from that planet. Until now the planet was unknown to many people outside of the governmental research team and it shows that most of the system is still uncharted and it was impossible to locate the origin of the alien creature. But in truth, the origins of the alien creature could have come from where the unmanned probe had crashed onto the mysterious planet. Strange note any and all information that can be gathered from the alien creature must be able to be useful in order to destroy all alien creatures from the alien invasion force plus also the alien creature inside

118

the quarantine area. All information from the first moment when the first alien creature was captured by the secret society until now when the alien invasion force has shown up to harm mankind. In understanding how life works with different people all over the world can be different in every way. When it comes to the people lives around the world. There are three different status levels in the modern age, but in truth, there are only really two levels of status. The two levels of status are rich and poor because the gap between the middle class and the poor are being erased as we speak.

It has been said for a long time now by many people that it will get worse before it will get better. With this understanding in the worst case scenario, the death of mankind and also the destruction of Earth is the final end of everything. Before this truly happens in our time period we each must face our greatest fear of all the survival of oneself. For the people that believe in God and Jesus truly wants to believe he will save us from harm when the time comes to meet him before the end of days.

When it comes time to fully understand how our lives could have been better if all of us in the world believe God is true. As our lives are connected in every way possible but in truth we are far more disconnected than ever before because of how each of us are blinded by the truth. For the time has finally been realized in all of its full understanding for reasons beyond our control and that was when the mysterious objects are in full view for the world to see. Once the mysterious objects are in full view we all fear for our lives will soon not be worth anything from this moment on.

This is no longer written in stories, graphic novels or even a fantasy book because an alien ship is now in the full view for anyone of us can see with our own eyes. In the bible, it states that in Revelations four horsemen will ride during the beginning of the end of days. The first to come towards mankind is war to everyone on Earth. War will leave people changed, dead or even infected by the blood of vengeance. The next will come is famine for those who will not survive because all of the food sources will be contaminated from the moment on when the war is over people will die of starvation. Then comes death but this death is totally different from all other deaths. Beyond war, famine and death come with a false understanding for a new leader shall lead us to a false victory.

Without war, each of us would not know our own strength to battle demons from hell that is coming to us within the mysterious alien spaceships. The demons that cause us to fear the truth that we are truly not alone in the universe from that moment on the alien spaceships entered into Earth's orbit gave mankind something to worry about until the whole world has made a choice on what to do about the approaching doom. How can the people of the world allow their own government to make the right decision about the safety of the world? What demise does mankind have in store for their survival now?

CHAPTER
24

AS THE MYSTERIOUS OBJECTS are now in the full view of every single satellites and signal stations around the world and even though the different governments around Earth sent the last of their rockets and missiles towards the different mysterious objects in the sky. As the few rockets and missiles that were left are flying through the sky something strange had happened to a few of them. The strange thing that had happened was a few of them exploded even before they encountered the mysterious objects in the sky. When the rockets and missiles hit their targets only a few were destroyed which were the smaller mysterious objects. Mysteriously the larger mysterious objects seemed to be unaffected by the rockets and also the missiles flying towards them. From the sky to the ground the falling debris is hitting everything in sight because of what the rockets and missiles hit and now there are multiple impact areas. For unknown reasons the smaller mysterious objects were causing a whole lot of damage when they dropped to the ground after being hit by the missiles and rockets. It seemed that every part each of the smaller mysterious objects would explode again once they hit any object on the ground. Besides the falling debris exploding when they came into contact with anything on the ground and the whole are looked like a mine field that had caused mass destruction. Building being destroyed and people are being killed all around the world by the exploding debris falling from the sky. The different governments ha finally decided to join forces around the world to protect Earth and its people from harm. Even though a lot of people have already died around the world from the exploding debris it seems more will die once the alien invasion starts.

The people of the world now realize the different governments around the world have been hiding the ultimate truth. The ultimate truth is that they knew in advance about the alien creature race and origins. With every known military base around the world has been called into action to prevent anyone from being harmed. Out comes the truth to finally show itself to the whole world because now the full truth is in front of them for the entire world to see. As the alien spaceships get closer to Earth's atmosphere no one can contain the lies anymore that has been spread all across the world for a long time now. More lies are being told on a daily basis and they are that everything will be alright and there is nothing to worry about in the near future. The main question that is being asked, "Why did we fire nuclear missiles on each other?"

Word has gotten out about what is truly happening around the quarantine area that the survivors are being killed for trying to leave the quarantine area without being examined. In truth they are being killed they are infected with some type of virus that is unknown to the government. Now no one is safe from their own government because for the fear of being killed just for interacting with any survivors from the quarantine area. The group of survivors that are being reduced by the military and the alien creature that is still within the quarantine area. Time is growing shorter for those on Earth and in the quarantine area the time a come for the Protectors of Earth to emerge from hiding and show themselves to the world. At first the small group of survivors that were left in the quarantine area had finally found shelter that no one knew about until a single person with no type of survival gear or weapons emerged from an entry way hidden by a mysterious staircase leading down under the ground. Only one word was spoken and that single word was safety they had no choice but to follow the mysterious person down under ground for their own safety.

The single Protector of Earth lead the small group of survivors to where all of the five hidden villages that were formed over five centuries ago to protect humans from being harmed in any way possible. The Protectors of Earth had slowly been tracking down survivors and sending them down to the underground fortress for protection against the military and the alien creature still hunting the lonely survivors. Since the activation of the nuclear warheads a few days ago around the world the survivability rate for mankind had decreased by eighty percent. The alien invasion attack force has started ending spaceships and troops down to Earth. It is clear that the attack has begun and everyone is in harm's way, but now is the time for the Protectors of Earth to fight and kill all alien creatures. Strangely the landing area for the spaceships and troops is none other than the meteor impact area inside the quarantine area. The battles between the alien creatures, human military personnel and the Protectors of Earth will have a lot of casualties on all side of the war. Strangely now the military has the fair advantage over the alien attack invasion force because of where they had landed.

The landing coordinates seems to be pointless but also at the same time, it shows how the alien attack invasion force does not care about the well-being of others during the battles. They are drawn to the meteor impact site for some strange reason but without knowing why the military surrounds the alien attack invasion force and starts firing upon them once they leave their spaceships. When the military opened fire upon the alien creatures none of them fell down to the ground and died because they seem to grow in size every time a bullet or any other ammunition had hit them during the gun battle. The bigger the alien creatures grow and the stronger they become and now the alien creature return fire from their own weapons and every single human that had fired upon the landing party were killed instantly by a unknown weapon that only left skeletal remains behind. Every one of the attacking human force were killed instantly because they were no match for the alien creature's weapon. Now is the time for the Protectors of Earth to show themselves and begin the fight that will eventually lead the humans towards surviving this event and many more in their own future.

When the Protectors of Earth appeared around the alien attack invasion force they noticed some marking on the alien creatures they have seen before on the main alien creature that was kept in the secret bunker. The marking shown were the same one that were on the five teachers from the future that were sent back in time to train the Protectors of Earth. So now it has come full circle the five teachers and the alien creatures are from the same home world that has been fighting for millions of years. Now the feud between the two races has come to Earth to either enslave all races on Earth or to kill everyone and move on. The weapons and armor from both the Protectors of Earth and the alien attack invasion force are equal in every way possible.

Even human the alien creature encountered that was not protected died by the alien creatures in the area but now the alien creatures realized there are some lesser alien creatures around the world that needs to be transformed into a normal alien creature. More and more spaceship full of troop is unloading more alien creatures on Earth every hour on the hour. The time has come to fully engage the humans and destroy them all. As the alien attack invasion force has spread out across the area to find every last human and kill them. For those humans that is not considered worthy of becoming an alien creature for the cause of gathering resources. Henceforth from this day forward it will be a fight for survival from all humans that are left alive during the attack.

CHAPTER
25

AFTER THE ATTACK ON the mysterious objects and that is when the aliens sent a mass attack towards Earth to destroy all things on Earth. When the government realized what they did it was too late for stopping any other attacks. The alien race also realized that the Earth's population is still big enough to ensure deaths on both sides of the war. It has come to the attention of the alien's that the alien creature that was sent to Earth centuries ago failed on its mission. In all honesty, the aliens were not ready for any type of resistance because they should have died off over the centuries that it took for them to travel from planet to planet.

In understanding the different strategies for conquering the different planets is to weaken the population first and then clean out the rest of the living population of the world. The technology in every possible area has ensured the survival of life because no matter what life holds a strong presence within most humans. It has come to the attention of most people on Earth that in order to survive they must defend themselves. The Earth's survival has always depended on how the world population reacts towards annihilation. The fear of dying becomes great because most people want to live and survive to live another day in this world.

One man especially realized that no matter what happens to the people of this world he will not be alone at the end. Meaning there will be a group of people believing in God to save them from annihilation and to ensure them they will survive. If they do not survive the war between them and the aliens they will go to heaven believing that their life had some type of meaning. As the alien spaceship headed toward Earth the government ensured them they had powerful enough weapons to destroy any alien invasion. As the spaceships got closer to the Earth more nuclear missiles were fired from every country around the world and even the ones that were hiding nuclear weapons for years.

As the people watched the missiles head towards the alien spaceships they had seen something that was astonishing, and that was how the spaceships disappear and reappeared once all the missiles had passed them. The alien spaceship came closer and closer to Earth and then smaller spaceships were released into the Earth's atmosphere to destroy all objects on the ground before any alien ground troops are released. As the smaller ships were attacking our own planes flew into the air to shoot down the alien's smaller ships, but also at the same time, the destroyed alien's ship was falling to the ground and destroying things on the ground as they crashed. People were running and hiding but most realized nothing could help them because of the destructive power as the alien ships were destroying every building they crashed into while falling to the ground. The smaller alien ships were not disappearing and reappearing like the bigger one's did for the missiles.

The government also realized that something else was happening on the ground other than the smaller spaceships destroying things. The things that were happening on the ground were more strange alien creatures appearing around some of the military bases. Instead of fighting the alien's in the air now they have to fight them on land because the government wanted to study the first alien creature they found a long time ago in the early 1500's. The secret is out finally that the government kept a secret hidden underground bunker that held an alien creature that can kill or transform humans into the same type of alien creature that was attacking Earth. Finally something even any government cannot cover up in a thousand years by saying what alien invasion there has never been an alien invasion because we are still here and alive.

There is no time to worry about cover up right now because the world is about to be annihilated for all eternity due to the fact that no one wanted to ensure or believe there were no aliens that could destroy us. The next step of the alien's attack plan is to send ground troops to annihilate all beings on Earth, but the reason behind this was simple to the alien's attack Earth. The resources that were needed to further more invasions of other planets that are inhabited by other creatures. The world was broadcasting about the millions of alien creatures on the ground killing and destroying everything in sight. The military is facing the alien creatures head on but losing ground very fast because it seems for every one alien killed in action another three takes its place. After battles by planes and other air crafts with the alien ships it all comes down to hand and hand combat plus other types of fighting strategies.

Every time a platoon of soldiers takes over an area the aliens come back with more troops to overtake the area again because the dead humans are changed into the alien creatures. Strangely enough bullets, knives, and other low-level weapons only inflict pain in which does not kill any of them. Rockets and other nuclear weapons kill them perfectly, but the only way to destroy them all is to fully attack the bigger spaceships so no smaller ships come down to Earth. The U.S. government brings out the new weaponry that was made just for these alien creatures because of all the different testing done on other test subjects throughout the development stages. Another strange factor about the alien creatures they only kill the children and change them at all, but another factor to the solution of the alien mass attack is to have a final last resort. The last resort would be to activate all unused nuclear warheads deep in the ground to ensure that no other inhabitable planet deals with the pain and struggles from the alien attacks.

The battle increases between the humans and the aliens because no one wants to be weak and call a truce for the lives on both sides of the war. The aliens seek annihilation and the humans seek survival, but now the humans realize that long distance space travel is possible with the technology of the alien spaceship. That would mean to steal an alien spaceship and figure out how to work it but multiple problems have arisen from this scenario. One problem they do not have time for is to wait because they are losing the war against the alien creatures, but another problem is what if one or more of the alien creatures are needed to fly the alien spaceship. It seems the only way for Earth to survive is to ensure every human being on Earth able to carry weapons is to be involved in the battle to save mankind.

Every person above the age of fifteen must fight for survival and freedom for the whole entire planet because it is the only way to survive the war. The peace and tranquility have left the world and now is replaced by cruelty and vengeance because of how the alien creatures deemed us as worthless and stupid sub-humans and not worth saving. As the war dragged on for days to weeks to months it finally hit the one year mark of when the alien creatures first approached Earth for the invasion. The alien creatures are getting very tired of this war but the different mass invasions are going to take place they need every resource that each planet holds to satisfy their home planet survival. The alien creature's home planet is so far away that it took them 1,000 Earth years to travel that distance but knowing this the understanding that only help for the alien creatures will not come in time. Understanding this concept a solution became available that every spaceship except one must be destroyed so this time around humans will have the advantage of space travel for our own purpose of destroying the alien creature's home planet.

One problem still remains how they could destroy all but one of the bigger alien spaceships if it disappears and reappears every time a nuclear missile is fired at the ships and the answer to that question was simple in itself. The answer would be to load the nuclear bombs onto the smaller ships that dock with the larger ships when it needs more supplies, but the nuclear weapons must be able to explode when and only when the nuclear bombs are on the bigger ships. In order to pull this off is by using the Trojan horse trick from our own history books. The Trojan horse trick needs to be put in place in order for the alien creatures to steal the crate and bring it aboard their own ships. All nuclear bomb crates will be marked food supplies with added symbol to let everyone know bombs are inside the crate, but also, the right information must be in the crate if anyone of the alien creatures can read the different Earth's languages.

The military put a dozen crates near a mass area of alien creatures so they could inspect them so they could realize that the humans need these crates to survive the war. The first of the dozen crates was loaded onto the smaller ship and transported to the awaiting bigger spaceship that was above the city. Once the crate was transported to the bigger ship a sensor was triggered on the ground below which told the military their crate was aboard the bigger spaceship. An hour went by and finally a loud explosion occurred from the bigger alien spaceship and the reason for this was because the crate was opened to be inspected by the alien creatures. Before any of the alien creatures knew what was happening eleven of the twelve bigger spaceships were destroyed by high power nuclear bombs, but the last crate had military personnel inside and waiting to take control of the last spaceship.

It seemed to take forever for the last bigger alien spaceship to be dealt with and come to find out the last crate was not opened until the next morning. The elite military group stood ready to battle for the last big spaceship and to take over the ship in which will turn the tides of the war. A few minutes after the crate was opened the elite military group attacked the alien creatures aboard the spaceship. Two hours later the attack on the spaceship was over and the elite military group took over and notified the ground troops the mission was a success. One problem arose from taking over the alien spaceship and that was a person must be plugged into the ships control in order to fly the ship. There are only three people left from the elite military group because of the alien creatures were stronger than the other that are on the ground.

The commander of the elite military group took action and place himself into the control center of the ship and once he did that his body was encased into the control system. The ship answered to his commands and landed the big spaceship into a secret hanger that no one knew about because he had to deliver the space ship in one piece for the scientists to study. Meanwhile, people were trying to kill the other alien creatures in the smaller spaceships and on the ground. It took another few months to wipe out the rest of the alien creatures that were still on the ground fighting and not realizing that the bigger spaceships were destroyed already. Everybody on Earth realized that the only way to ensure every alien creature was destroyed is to find the hottest degree that they burn at and will not be able to recover from the heat of any fire and hopefully they die.

CHAPTER
26

AN ALL-OUT WAR BETWEEN Earth and the Alien's for world domination. Ending the war between humans and the alien creatures will be difficult because they are motivated by greed and persistence for survival. Now is the time to find all the smaller spaceships to destroy them and to use all the leftover pieces for their own need of space travel to the alien creature's home planet. It is time to kill every last alien creature that is still on Earth for reasons beyond their own control. The main reason behind this is to ensure the survival of all humans that are left on Earth. No more samples of alien DNA will be left on Earth for reasons of protecting everyone on Earth and also the products that were made from the alien creature DNA will be destroyed. Also, tests will be given to everyone on Earth to ensure all alien creatures DNA is removed from their bodies and on Earth.

After the alien bigger spaceship was taken over by the elite military group to the hidden military base the spaceship will be inspected and studied until all aspects of the alien spaceship is well documented. The smaller versions of the bigger spaceships are being used to be fully understood and used as spare parts for the bigger alien spaceship. What cannot be used for spare parts will be melted down and used to build another spaceship for the human kind of space travel. Meaning the use and understanding of the new metals from the alien creature home world will be used in understanding how to beat them on their own home planet without getting anyone killed. The computer control will not be like the alien creature spaceship but like a normal ship with seats, consoles for controls and sleeping quarters aboard the spaceship. All this will take more time to build because of how much knowledge is needed for the construction of any new spaceships for attack and exploring outer space.

Our world continues to grow every day around us, but at the same time, some of us do not have the time to take solace to see what is around us in our lives. When it is too late to see what is around us, and then our ways of life is threatened because of our greed and sins. Our greed motivates us to work and spend our lives to acquire things we do not need in our lives. In the future if we continue on our course each of us will not have enough time to realize how much of our lives have passed by without truly at what needs to be seen. In truth when people look around, they see nothing but being able to survive our world without sacrificing our values in life.

One more truth about our world and it may be hard to understand due to the fact each of us is blinded by our views of the world. The fact is unless we acknowledge our problems within our lives we will never realize the problems our world is truly facing because of greed and our sins. Each of us has greed and sins compulsions due to how we believe our lives should be lived, but at the same time, our eyes and minds are affected by the lies the government tells each of us every day. Over the years, the population in the world is growing rapidly, because of the development in modern medicine that prolongs life. Soon enough the world's population will far exceed the resources for survival because when people outweigh resources there is no way for survival in this world. In the not so near future, the fate of mankind hangs in the balance, because the world's population has expanded greatly.

For the past twenty years, the world's resources have been getting less and less, because a lot of people have been using more of their resources to acquire the things they want which in the long run they do not need them. Meaning each person has enough resources will last for one hundred years unless the government deems you worthless then your life resources are forfeited and given to another person.

In the year of 2050, the world has come together to deal with the world's population, and the reason for this is because the world's population is now close to nine billion people. The only downside to this new system is who gets to watch over the people to make sure who is worthless or who is deemed with giving resources to when they are born. The Council of Life which comprises of thirteen members from the richest part of the world. The system worked just fine until the year 2060 because rich people understood how to beat the system. In 2060, the Council of Life became corrupt, because they would make people that were perfect for the system into worthless people. The Council of Life will be blinded by lust and greed with good credits and abundance of gold and silver. When this comes to light the one that had committed adultery will become known and in return will be given dishonor and removed from the Council of Life. All due to the fact rich people wanted to live longer, and also they wanted all lower class people to die.

Once the corruption was uncovered it was too late for the people the Council of Life had changed a lot of people from perfect to worthless. Seven hundred people that have been deemed worthless by the Council of Life have been captured. Half of them will be murdered, but that will stop after the fifteenth person dies. The worthless will be seized and plunged into a tub of sulfur in which they are forced to drink and die. At the end when the Council of Life was found corrupt all the council people locked their own selves into the palace. In the palace where the great Council of Life stays the people inside are trapped, because of their choices they were making to thin out the world's population. Without fully realizing the Council of Life left the world in worst shape then it has ever been in many years. Within the next year or two if resources did not rebound back to normal for supplying the world population with food they will starve to death. Meaning without controlling all resources there will not be enough food or other resources to maintain the world's population.

In the year, 2062 resources on Earth is getting low, because the world's population has grown to over ten billion people. The greatest famine in history is vast approaching, but it will start out in the rural areas then grow into the major cities around the world. The famine will be so great that people will resort to eating people, and they will also grab the roots from trees to eat them.

True most things can be synthesized by all humans, but one thing that cannot be grown fast enough is food. There are only about a dozen farms left that can grow food because other farms are dried up and useless. The U.S. Government had found a way to make a mass amount of food but they are missing a key element in the process. The government can synthesize about 0.05 oz. in one month time, because the element is harmful to animals but not harmful to humans. The element is called grondpila-128, because of one reason it looks like a cross between sugar and flour. Grondpila-128 formations are crystals with snowflake designs.

Scientists have been trying to find a better and faster way to make this element, but no luck at all. Then one scientist realized they had a better way to make the element, but that was not an option yet. The reason being is because the only planet that has a remote chance of making this element was passes the dwarf planet called Pluto. A new Council was formed to find a way to the planet for collecting the element to bring back to Earth, and for their pending survival. Under the rule of the new Council five of the seven kingdoms will merge to become as one, but the other two will not follow because of corruption. The new Emperor will enter into the new city after they merge, but the newly formed kingdom will be attacked by the other two kingdoms that did not join the union. The new Emperor will leave after the attack to keep far from the enemy that attacked the new kingdom. The new Emperor left before he could be killed by the enemies of the other two kingdoms that wished to harm him different ways. The new enemies will free the falsely accused that spoke out against the new kingdom.

When five of the seven kingdoms combined to make one large kingdom a lot of people were happy about everything, but at least the other two kingdoms did not approve of the merger. For many reasons they did not feel as they were not wanted in the new kingdom at all. The many reasons behind their understanding were simple. Firstly, they were not higher class of people and had no opinion that matter in the merger. Secondly, they were continuously low on resources and had to steal or borrow resources to survive. Thirdly, they were over populated of the old style Council meaning it was where the worthless people went to live after the old Council deemed them worthless in the first place. Fourthly, the land they lived on could be stripped of resources in the new kingdom to help the new kingdom to survive longer in the world. Lastly, they did not have enough education value among them to help in any way to the new kingdom. Meaning they were worthless and they needed to die so their resources could be transferred to the new kingdom. The two other kingdoms did attack the newly formed kingdom, but only to release all the falsely accused people that were against the new formation of the five kingdoms of one major kingdom. For attacking the new kingdom the Emperor decided to attack the two other kingdoms and destroy them forever and not one of them will be left alive to say anything about what happened during the battle.

The Emperor announced, "The two other kingdoms will not survive the battle because they are all lower class people with no regard for political agendas. The two kingdoms do not understand how important it is by working to together for the greater good of the planet Earth. These are a few reasons as to why they must be destroyed so we can continue to survive in this world of ours." The new kingdom attacked the two other kingdoms to destroy and kill all who lived in the two kingdoms. The new kingdom surrounds both of the other two kingdoms to destroy them once and for all, but on the second night, a few of the best warriors exited the two other kingdoms to massacre the approaching army. Strangely enough, the camp for the new kingdom army was empty of soldiers, and as the few warriors entered into the camp they realized it was a trap for them. The true campsite was on the other side of the two kingdoms, but before the few warriors got back to their kingdoms everyone was killed and all the buildings were burned to the ground. When the few warriors entered back into their kingdoms a thousand troops were waiting for them, and as they entered into the cities all of them were killed instantly. The war between the newly formed kingdom and the other two kingdoms were over in one single night. The Emperor was a fierce warrior himself, because of the teachings and learning as he grew up through the ages of technology. Over the next several months the Emperor began to wipe away all traces of the other two kingdoms as they were never there in the first place. To him the only kingdom worth anything is the newly formed kingdom that he had made into one so all the people in the world now has a place to call home.

CHAPTER 27

THE WORLD PULLED TOGETHER enough resources to finally build a transport ship that can travel in that distance and back within six months. Due to the approaching famine soon the transport ship will approach an unknown port in the far distant galaxy. Also in that time period they have to travel, mine and then return to Earth before all the resources run out. One of the many problems is the speed of the ship, and also the carrying capacity load of the ship. The world only has three years of resource left and that includes food for the whole world. That is how much resources are left after one transport ship was built, because they could not spare any more resources to the cause at saving the world.

The crews for the ship comprise of military, scientists, miners, flight crew and also transport crew. Each person has a specific duty on the ship for assurance of a safe return to Earth. The ship will be launched in four days' time, because of the short window of good weather. Two days away from take off another problem arises, and that problem was the guidance system and the navigation system. For the next 36 hours they worked on both systems to working status, but with one problem the guidance had a patch program well enough until the crew had a chance to repair it on the trip to the planet. Finally one hour countdown to liftoff, and everything that is needed for the trip was on the ship beforehand. Every crew member for the ship prepared to board the ship at two hours before liftoff. At the twenty minute mark all was ready for the trip, but one extra-large crate was brought aboard for emergencies only.

It will take two months there two months to mining and then two months traveling back to Earth. This is the schedule only if nothing happens during the trip, but if something happens hopefully the trip will not take more than a year tops. One minute to liftoff all systems checks are green and a go for launch. Liftoff has occurred as the ship blast off towards outer space the speed of the ship is way faster than any other ships or rockets in the past. This finally passed through Earth's atmosphere and on the way towards the planet passed Pluto.

The fuel for the ship is self-reproducing formula, and as the days go by the guidance and the navigation programs were recalculated and functioning correctly for the trip now. All was going great until day 15 and on that day they activated the special engine drive to get to the destination of the trip on time. Once the final code was inputted into the computer the special engine drive was activated and space and time was warped. Even though space and time was warped everyone on and including the ship was still in real time. The ship picked up speed even though normal time was 24 hours in a day, but outside the ship time and space had no meaning and no concept.

After two hours has passed all was well, but unfortunately the special engine drive shut down. As the ship comes to a stop the crew brings up the navigation system and the reading shows unknown location and time. As the calculations were made for the new location, and it was determined they were stuck in between normal space and time versus alternate space and time. Come to find out the special engine drive was nothing new, because it was salvaged from an old Alien spaceship that crash back in the early 20th century. It was a race against time because Earth needs our help to be saved.

When the ship and the crew is stuck in an alternate space and time a signal was sent out once the special engine drive was activated. The signal alerted the Alien race that one of their vessels that were lost a long time ago was finally coming home. The vessel was moving and now it stopped, because the signal was no longer activated. The Alien race sent a rescue ship to help them the rest of the way home. The crew realized something was wrong and it was time for the special extra-large crate to be opened. But first all other possibilities must be dealt with, and no other hope for survival then the special extra-large crate can be opened as a last resort. Systems on the ship are malfunctioning all over because of the alternate space and time. As the special extra-large crate is moved out of storage and accessed within the next hour or two, because there are no other way around the problem if the ship is not working.

The military part of the crew opened the special extra-large crate and noticed another special engine drive with all mechanical parts plus a small arsenal of weapons. Hopefully the scientists and the other crew members can replace the new special engine drive before anyone not human shows up around them. The radar system is actually working and started making a noise when the radar made contact with an incoming Alien ship. The crew prepared and rushed to put the new special engine drive into the ship. It took over an hour to fully install the new special engine drive, and the ship's computer that is controlled by the special engine drive activated an emergency maneuver out of the alternate space and time. Once the ship was back in normal space and time all readings showed with the new location and date. The new location shows the ship is just about half way to their destination, and the date is October 30, 1962. Two choices have to be made: one go back to Earth and warn them of the pending doom of mankind, or continue on with the mission to the planet for the special element?

The only choice the crew now had to make was to identify how and why they went back in time to achieve their mission. Either option was not allowed because if they did go back to Earth they would change history either for the best or worst in which will end up being a paradox. Since it was 1962 the time has come to head towards the alien creature home planet to stop an all-out war between them and the humans. Finally the choice was made the military took over command of the spaceship and started towards the home planet of the alien creatures that will soon try to destroy all of mankind in the process. With the new special engine given each of them time to figure out on how to proceed with the new mission. In order to proceed with the new mission the first thing must be understood by everyone on the spaceship and that was the mission parameters had changed because now is the time to attack the alien creatures before they arrived at Earth. They all agreed and set course towards the alien creature home planet for now mankind will stop or even attack the alien creatures before they had a chance to annihilate all human beings.

Now the crew members also realized that since the mission parameters was changed this is now a one way mission with no possible way of going back to their time and Earth. Meaning they now have to find the fastest way possible to the alien creature planet or meet them at some point in time to finish the attack. Since the time and space they come from does not exist yet now is the time to make all attempts to stop any attack force heading towards Earth. Even though there is still one alien creature on Earth it will have to be dealt with at a later time. The understanding of how time factors or as other put it a temporal paradox between normal and alternative space and time space travel.

In order to maintain the spaceship to travel the actual distance between Earth and the alien creature home planet the spacecraft must follow the direct path towards the alien creature home world. In doing so they must also be prepared for anything that comes their way but also the travel time will have to be reduced in order to find them in time. The understanding of how they travel through space is the key factor of knowing where they will be during their travels towards Earth at this very moment in time. The concept of meeting the alien invasion force is the only possibility that will be met with less arguing then allowing the alien creatures anywhere near Earth. With the charts from the taken over spaceship from the alien creatures showed where exactly the course and speed of the alien invasion force. Now is the time to match the speed and course to find them once and for all.

As the information is inputted into the ship computer the special engine drive was activated and ship took off like a bat out of hell. For some strange reason once the ship was turned into the military warship the speed had been increased by seventy-five percent. Meaning it is taking less time to intercept the alien creature invasion force than planned and also it will be a surprise to everyone onboard the warship if they do survive. Survivability has now increased by tenfold because with the new speed of the warship all of its tactical offensive weapons are now armed for full combat readiness. Finally the time has come to turn the tides of war to save all of mankind from annihilation and also to show that no matter what humans endure throughout life they will overcome with the understanding they will succeed.

When the timer hit three hours until attack time everyone on the warship scrambled to their positions aboard the warship to prepare for battle. Before they realized all of the alarms aboard the warship went off because of the approaching alien creature's spaceship heading towards them. The warship made all stop to encounter the approaching alien invasion force and made another realization that there were more alien spaceships this time around than before for some strange reasons that were unknown to the people from Earth. The truth is finally shown and the time has come to engage the enemy until either all of the enemy spaceships is destroyed or the human warship is destroyed.

Before the enemy was able to take any action the warship attacked the lead ships to show force in which three of the alien spaceships were destroyed. Now the alien spaceships changed direction to run away from their own pending doom of being annihilated. After the alien spaceships turned to escape they noticed that the attacking warship was human in nature. As the human warship chased the alien spaceships to destroy them they had to figure out how humans are able to travel in space. The knowledge of how would greatly reduce the chances for humans to develop this type of technology again in life.

Two more alien spaceships were now destroyed and they are now down to eight in all, but how are the humans able to track them in space. Strange enough the bigger alien spaceships are not sending out the smaller ships to attach the human warship. Now is the time to destroy the human warship and proceed towards Earth. Even before the alien spaceships had time to deploy a way to destroy the human warship all of a sudden the human warship destroyed another three alien spaceships. Now the true understanding of how each of the alien spaceships are being hunted down and destroyed before they could even reach Earth to annihilate all of mankind. This warship is from the future and parts of the warship were salvaged from the wreckage of alien debris that was left behind in the attack.

The alien creature attack force sounded the alarm to retreat because they were outnumbered and being destroyed from a ship that is from Earth future. The faster each of the alien spaceships tried to run away they were gunned down in the wake of carnage. Now the last alien spaceship was left to destroy before it could head back to their home planet for warning them of the pending doom that is heading towards them in a hurry. Right before the alien spaceship turned to escape one last time the last three missiles were fired upon them and destroyed the last remaining alien spaceship. Finally the mission is finished and completed now is the time to return home even though the year is now 1962.

Printed in the United States
By Bookmasters